THE
EGYPTIAN
BOX

JANE LOUISE CURRY

THE
EGYPTIAN
BOX

SCHOLASTIC INC.
New York Toronto London Auckland Sydney
Mexico City New Delhi Hong Kong Buenos Aires

No part of this publication may be reproduced, stored in a retrieval system, or transmitted in any form or by any means, electronic, mechanical, photocopying, recording, or otherwise, without written permission of the publisher. For information regarding permission, write to Margaret K. McElderry Books, Simon & Schuster Children's Publishing Division, 1230 Avenue of the Americas, NY, NY 10020.

ISBN 0-439-80625-9

12 11 10 9 8 7 6 5 4 3 2 1   5 6 7 8 9 10/0

Printed in the U.S.A.   40

First Scholastic printing, September 2005

Book design by Abelardo Martínez
The text for this book is set in Janson.

for Margaret McElderry

(and with thanks to Sue Bridgewater)

ONE

Tee Woodie, sitting in the fifth row of the Oasis Empire theater, watched the screen in a trance. Her fingers felt at the bottom of the jumbo tub for the last handful of popcorn, and fumbled it into her mouth. Like Princess Maryam, up on the screen, she looked in dismay from the princely green-cloaked figure in the middle of the palace courtyard to the short, pudgy young man in purple pantaloons who peered out from behind him. *That* was the real Prince Farad? If it was, Tee wondered, who was the tall, handsome one Maryam was in love with? On the screen, Princess Maryam was asking the same question. *"If that silly puppy is the prince, who are you?"*

Whoever he was, he was growing taller by the minute. Maryam, the dweeby real Prince Farad, and Tee in the audience all stared as he grew, until he towered as high as the palace gates.

"*I? I am the unhappy djinn Fasilbar, who was servant to this Farad.*"

A "djinn"? . . . A *genie?* But—but he had been such a wonderful Prince Farad of Allibas! He had rescued Maryam the sweetmeat-seller from her wicked master, and revealed that she was the daughter, stolen as a child, of the Caliph of Khaibar. He was kind, and brave, and funny. He was a *genie?* And now that he had granted Farad's last wish, he was free, and returning to the Mountains of the Afreet?

As the djinn Fasilbar touched the jewel in his turban, bowed, and vanished, Tee clasped her hands over her breastbone and tucked her chin down against them, afraid almost to breathe. Why hadn't Maryam *said* something? But—wait. Now she was pushing the doofus Farad away and calling out loudly for her horse. Tee drew in her breath as Maryam sprang onto the saddle. "*Why? Why?*" the poor, pudgy Farad was asking.

"*Why? Because you are not the Farad who won me. If Fasilbar the Djinn could be a man once, now he can be one again, and for good!*"

Then her golden horse sprang through the gates, and she was racing out through the moonlit city and onto the silver road that led to the Terrible Mountains of the Afreet.

THE END.

At the fade-out, Tee wasn't the only one in the audience who jumped up and cheered, but she sat down again quickly, embarrassed, even though there were other cheers and hoots and applause, and a scattered boo or two. Seats banged up. There was the usual bustle of a crowded Saturday afternoon audience gathering up belongings, stretching, talking, and shuffling sideways toward the aisles. Tee sat with her eyes closed, spellbound, while the names of actors and makeup artists and electricians and camel herders and parrot trainers rolled up the screen. The music swelled around her, and she did not open her eyes until the last note faded away and the lights came up. Most of the audience had already filed out. Tee sighed, brushed salt and popcorn crumbs from her shorts, and stood. Chin in the air and shoulders straight, she moved along the row to join the stragglers. With a Princess Maryam flick of her bushy ponytail, she moved up the aisle with Maryam's gliding, graceful walk toward the real world. And smack into it.

The boy ahead of her let the door swing back without looking behind him.

Tee, still dreaming her way across the moonlit desert, woke up just in time to catch at the door's edge and dodge sideways. Off-balance, she tripped on a worn carpet edge and fell facedown on the lobby's blue-carpeted floor with her nose on a yellow star.

Everyone in the lobby turned to look. Tee saw all their feet turn in her direction, and her face burned scarlet with embarrassment. She scrambled to her knees to gather up the sunglasses, the half bag of peanuts, and the video of *Dragonheart*, and other bits and pieces that had spilled from her shoulder bag.

One young woman crossed the lobby to her. "Are you okay?" she asked.

Ignoring the ticket-taker's grin and the smothered giggles from a group of boys and girls her own age, Tee clambered to her feet. "I'm fine," she muttered. Looking straight ahead, she marched frozen-faced out through the exit doors.

For a moment the sudden, dazzling glare outside made the world look white. The oven-blast of heat left Tee breathless. She squeezed her eyes shut until she could find the sunglasses in her bag and fumble them on. River Street was almost empty. Most of the movie-goers had vanished into the Burger Boy next door, probably, or the South State Road bus just pulling away from the curb, or into Hersey's General Store. Her father's car was nowhere in sight.

Tee scowled. He had *promised*. He and her mother had a meeting with Great-uncle Sebastian's lawyer— something about more junk he had left them in his will. That couldn't have taken more than half an hour, and then they would have gone home for lunch. Tee herself had an early lunch at Burger Boy before the movie. Why didn't he *come?* It was the last Saturday before school started, and now it was spoiled.

Sweat slid down the sides of her nose to dry before it reached her chin. With each drop that dripped she felt sorrier for herself. She longed to be back in Maine. She hated summer in Oasis Wells. She would never get used to the desert. She hated the heat. She hated the glaring, shimmering air, and the town it hung over. She hated the way it dried her hair into a frizzy bush. *He. Had. Promised.*

It was too hot and too far to walk to Look and Listen!, the video shop her father had inherited from Great-uncle Sebastian along with the house and junk shop. Besides, Look and Listen! was in the opposite direction from home. He might not even be there. *Telephone.* That was it. Phone first. Tee didn't remember seeing a telephone in the lobby. Not that it mattered whether there was or wasn't. She wasn't going back in. Not to ask that spotty-faced ticket-taker, and have him grin at her again.

She decided to try the County Public Library. She knew there was a phone behind the checkout desk. The squat, square library, with thick walls plastered to look like adobe, was her favorite place. A lot of its books were old, or were paperbacks people had donated, but it was air-conditioned, and was only a block away. Tee shaded her eyes from the sun's glare with a hand held over the top of her sunglasses, and stepped out into the desert-hot brightness. By the time she reached the corner, she could feel the heat of the pavement scorching through the soles of her sandals.

Once through the library's front door, Tee closed her eyes and took a deep breath of the cool air. Then she headed for the water fountain. After a long drink, she gave a happy sigh of "Oo-oo-oh!" She didn't realize she had *oo-ooh*ed out loud until Mrs. Fuentes came out of the little office behind the checkout desk to shush her.

"Goodness, Tee!" she exclaimed when she saw who it was. "You're red as a boiled beet. Are you all right?"

Tee nodded. "My father was supposed to pick me up, and he didn't. Can I use the phone here?"

"It's not a public phone," Mrs. Fuentes said as she moved the telephone from the desk to the counter, "but you look as if you qualify as an emergency. I bet you'll be glad to get home to that nice, cool stone house. Old Mr. Fall once told me he had the outer walls built three feet thick. His 'castle,' he called it."

Tee stabbed her finger at the numbers on the dial and waited while the phone rang at home. "Maybe," she grumbled. "But it's weird. I miss our old house in Maine."

No one was at home in the old stone house. At the fourth ring, the answering machine clicked on, and

Tee's brother Charles's answerphone voice chirped, *"This is the Woodies'. If you'd like to leave a really-truly message for Sarah, Frank, Tee, or Charles, go ahead after the beep; if you're only trying to sell something, thank you and good-bye forever."* Tee phoned Look and Listen! next, but the Saturday sales clerk reported that Mr. Woodie had not been at the store all day. Mrs. Woodie had come in after lunch to do the restocking orders, but had gone out the door only two minutes ago. That left Great-uncle Sebastian's junk shop. Where the phone was disconnected. Great. She had to walk another block and a half.

"A block-and-a-half-long oven," Tee muttered. She hung up the receiver and pushed the phone across the counter as Mrs. Fuentes came back from the open shelves with a book in her hand.

"I ran across this on the shelves the other day. Have you seen it?"

Tee looked at the plastic-covered book jacket: *Were the Gypsies Egyptians?* by Sebastian Fall. She shrugged. "No. But my father says it's kind of crack-pottish." Like Great-uncle Sebastian himself, she thought to herself.

Mrs. Fuentes grinned. "Oh yes, so was he. He was interested in everything and anything. The parts in this about his travels are fun, though. But your phone call—was anyone at home?"

Tee sighed. "No. The only other place I can think of is the junk shop."

"Back out into the sun." Mrs. Fuentes made a sympathetic face, and then brightened. She stooped to rummage under the counter, and came up with a blue and yellow collapsible umbrella. "Use this. It's been in Lost and Found since last year, so no one will miss it. And good luck. If you don't find anyone at the shop, come back here and I'll give you a ride home at five."

In spite of the umbrella's help, Tee's T-shirt was sticking to her back, and the hair at the back of her neck was wet before she was halfway there. The junk shop! What could be important enough there to take almost four hours? It was a junk shop, for goodness' sake!

Great-uncle Bass, who left the shop to the Woodies, had died on the first of June, four days before his one hundredth birthday. All that his short will, written twenty years earlier, had said was, *"To great-great nephew Frank, the best of a boring bunch of Leticia's and my great-greats, I leave everything except my money in the bank, which is to go to The Society for the Preservation of Landmark Trees."*

The school year in Portland, Maine, was just over, so Mr. Woodie had quit his job at the hardware store, the family packed everything into a U-Haul van, left their rented house, and moved west. Tee had sulked all the way across the country, and after two and a half months was still unhappy. Great-uncle Bass's house was a half-hour bus ride outside of town. There were few close neighbors, and none with children. It wouldn't have helped if there were children. She was too shy to be good at making friends.

Yesterday, Great-uncle Sebastian's lawyer, Mr. Witt, had telephoned to say that he had found a recently handwritten postscript to the will tucked into an old account book, and could they meet at the junk shop today. According to Mr. Witt, the P.S. read, "*I have left my personal gifts to my family in the large Chin box in my treasure room.*"

Chin box. What on earth was a Chin box? And— "treasure room"? In some ratty old junk shop? That had to be a joke. As Tee hurried along the heat-shimmering sidewalk, she told herself she wasn't the least bit curious. She was only desperate to get out of the sun.

TWO

As Tee's father's great-great uncle by marriage, old Sebastian—"Bass" for short—Fall had been Tee and Charles's great-great-*great* uncle. Because three "greats" made an awkward mouthful, she and Charles and their parents always left off the last two. He had been a nice enough old man, Tee supposed, even if his clothes *were* all secondhand and never too clean. Both his clothes and he smelled cigarette-ish and—old. On one long—two months long—visit when Tee was eight to their old house in Maine, near Portland, he had been kind, and funny, she supposed, but she always felt uncomfortable with him there. Embarrassed, too. He was a scruffy old man with food stains on his neckties and shirtfronts. Charles, then six, had been fascinated by Great-uncle Bass ever since he heard his father describe him as an "old pack rat." Well, he *was* one. Or an old squirrel, maybe. He scrounged and scavenged, and squirreled away cast-off odds and ends from attics and garages that he was paid to clear out and cart away when people died or moved house. To Charles, already a fiendish collector of beetles and seashells, and tin boxes to keep them in, that had sounded like a great way to live.

Great Uncle Bass had lived alone. His wife, Leticia Woodie Fall, a tall, pretty, fair-haired girl and woman in the old family photos, died when Tee's father was small. Tee was named after her. Leticia Ann! Tee, only middling-tall, darker, and almost-but-not-quite pudgy, hated the name. It made her feel shorter, fatter, and plainer. "Tish" did, too, and "Letty" sounded like a character in some dusty old book about pioneers or girls who wore long skirts and bonnets and buttoned boots. For a while she spelled her name "Lateesha." It *looked* better that way, though it sounded almost the same. She had ended up with "Tee." She planned to change it when she was eighteen to Marcia or Tracy. No more Leticia. "Marcy." That was it: Marcy Woodie. Marcy Annetta Woodie.

The sign above the street window of Great-uncle Bass's shop read, THE DOWNSTAIRS ATTIC. In small letters under that, it said, SEBASTIAN FALL, PROP. A small, neat sign was taped to the window in the door.

CLOSED

All enquiries to

Chapman, Witt & Crumplesham,

Hample Street, Rock Spring

Tee closed the umbrella and knocked, but there was no answer. She tried the doorknob. It turned easily, so she pushed the door open far enough to peer into the gloom. She had never visited the shop. One look now was enough to tell her that it was every bit as dim and grungy as she expected. She wrinkled up her nose in distaste. The long, narrow room was dusty and cob-webbed, and its crooked aisles were lined with eerie, humped shapes. Tee's heart gave a jump, but a second look told her that the humps were tables and display cases covered by old sheets and ragged bedspreads. Off to the left, a stairway climbed up to a doorway with the word OFFICE in faded lettering.

"Daddy," Tee shouted. "Are you up there?" She stomped up the stairs to look, but the office was empty.

Downstairs again, she swept a scornful look around the room, but on her way back to the front door, curiosity got the better of her. She reached out and snatched the dusty sheet from the nearest hump. "Some treasure room!" She snorted.

The case was the old-fashioned glass-fronted dis-play kind. Its top shelf was a jumble. Cupless saucers were tumbled in together with salt-and-pepper-celler holders missing either salts or peppers, a beer stein with a broken lid, and battered tin pie plates. On the next shelf down, a bundle of old-style hotel coat hangers was wedged in on top of a tray holding a jumble of coat hooks, bolts without nuts, padlocks without keys, and strings of keys without locks. All junk. At the bottom were wick holders for oil lamps, and a collection of china doorknobs. A box held old souvenir bottle openers and two shoehorns. Half a dozen old wooden rulers read, SHOP AT HARLAND'S HABERDASHERY—ALWAYS A GOOD RULE. What on earth was a haberdashery?

Not everything was pure junk. On a nearby table she uncovered a handsome brass bowl and a pair of cast-iron elephant bookends. An Aladdin-style brass oil lamp, too. That made her blink and, in spite of herself, she was tempted to reach out and rub it. Instead, she frowned and called out loudly. "*ANY*body here? DADDY?" Where could he have gone?

Tee was out of ideas. The North State Road bus ran only once every three hours on Saturdays. The next one was due in—she looked at her watch—five minutes. The nearest bus stop was back by the library. She wavered. Then a faint thump behind her solved the mystery. A second dull *THUMP*, and a dim ghost of a cheer rose from somewhere below.

It took Tee a while to find the door to the basement

stairs. She discovered it at last in a small back room where a grimy sink and toilet were half hidden by tea chests, cartons, and old crates. These were stacked higgledy-piggledy everywhere, but left a narrow path to the open cellar door. Inside, a bare bulb lit the wooden stair steps. Tee clattered down them noisily.

"Daddy? Where are you?"

There was no answer.

A second bare bulb lit the basement room. It gave enough light to show that it was only the first of several low, cobwebby storerooms. A narrow passage threaded its way through the jumble in each room from one door to the next. Every foot of wall space was lined with crowded shelves, and the floors were heaped with dusty cartons. Some of those on top gaped open, revealing old books or toys, or dishes, or assortments of odds and ends. The basement air was cooler than in the room above, but that didn't make up for the spiderwebs. Tee made her way gingerly from the third room to a fourth with her nose wrinkled in distaste. She kept her arms crossed close to her body and her hands tucked in tightly. She *hated* spiderwebs.

"Daddy?"

"Princess?"

Tee peered into what looked like the last room of all. Her father's voice had seemed to come from there.

In the shadows along the right-hand wall, cartons were piled haphazardly onto broad shelves that reached almost to the ceiling. To the left, a sagging cupboard stood out at an angle from the wall. Beyond it, wooden chairs without seats were stacked up in teetery towers, but there was no sign of her father. The light was dim, but she saw what might be drag marks on the grime-black floor beside the cupboard. Nervously, she peered behind it.

"Tee? Come on in. All the way back," her father's voice called.

There *was* a doorway in the wall. When she slipped in behind the cupboard, Tee saw that the wooden door had been opened inward, into the darkness.

"Daddy?" she called doubtfully. "What's in there? Why are you in there in the dark?"

A beam of bright light flashed out through the door, and then her father's face appeared above the dazzle of the battery lantern he carried. "It's the coalhole. The old coal bin under the sidewalk. It's Great-uncle Bass's 'treasure room.' Come take a look at all we've discovered. We've found the mysterious 'Chin box,' too. Come on—you won't get dirty if you're careful."

Mr. Woodie's own face and neck were smudged and smeared with dust and grime. His shirt was dust-gray and sweaty. He looked, Tee thought impatiently, like somebody who lived in a cardboard box in a—well, in a coalhole. He *never* cared how he looked. At least, not when he was excited about something. "This way, Princess." He backed back into the old coalhole, shining the light on the floor at Tee's feet. "Look out for the boards there. They're from the big crate, and there are nails in some of 'em."

Tee balked. "I don't want to come in. *Dad*dy! You forgot. You were supposed to pick me up after the movie. I want to go *home*."

"Sure, sure. We will, we will. Five minutes. I promise. But take a look at this first. . . . Whoops, watch out for Mr. Witt." Four steps into the small, low-ceilinged room, Mr. Woodie propped the flashlight on top of a stack of crates. In its beam, Tee saw both the stout, dignified lawyer and her skinny little brother. As they turned toward her, their grimy faces were, like Mr. Woodie's, lit up by white-toothed grins. The glasses all three wore glittered. They looked like three gleeful chimney sweeps, she thought, as they hovered over the large, dark chest that sat inside the wreckage of a large crate. Tee ignored it and peered into the open box nearest her.

"Some treasures! A junky old plastic radio, and— *ugh!*—a platter with a fake *snake* curled up on it?"

Mr. Witt, the cleanest chimney sweep, protested. "No, no, my dear! The radio's a mint-condition nineteen-forties green catalin Fada Streamliner. Collectors pay amazing prices for such things. And the platter is an antique Italian majolica *piatta di pompa*. Worth thousands. At least, I believe it's antique, and not a copy. It must be. Sebastian would have known." He looked around and shook his head. "We will need to bring in experts to catalog all this. It's quite amazing."

Tee was impressed in spite of herself. Thousands of dollars? For an ugly plate? Reluctantly, she nodded toward the dark chest. "What's in there?" she asked.

"This?" Charles was almost hopping up and down with excitement. "This is *it*. The Chin box! Chin-Period-Box. Abbreviated. Chinese box! Get it? Were we dumb, or what!"

Their father moved the light so that Tee could see the intricate carving on the dark wooden chest's top and sides. Curled-up dragons slept on the pale wood medallions at the center of the top and of each of the side panels.

Tee peered inside. "Oh, wow! Newspaper!" she said sarcastically.

Mr. Witt only smiled. "Sebastian's favorite wrapping paper. For Christmas he used the colored comic-strip pages." He drew out a bulky, string-tied shape and read what was written on the scrap of white paper taped to it: " *'For young Charles, the Weird One.'* I take it that's you, young man? I'll cut the string, shall I? Be careful—it's heavy."

Charles rested the package on the rim of the chest and tore off the newspaper. Inside was a strange-looking machine with wheels and dials and keys, all made of brass. Engraved on the base was an oval medallion surrounded with delicate engraved scrollwork, but the space left for the inscription was empty.

"What on earth is it?" Mr. Woodie asked.

Mr. Witt wiped his forehead with a snowy handkerchief and ended up looking as if his bushy, gray eyebrows grew across the bridge of his nose. "I've no idea. Charles?"

"I don't know," Charles said. "Some kind of calculating machine, I think." He tipped it up to see if there might be another label or an explanation on the bottom. There wasn't.

"And Great-uncle Bass thought *you* were weird," Tee said scornfully. She picked up a much smaller parcel to squint at its label in the dim light, and gave a sudden giggle. "This one's for Cousin Frieda." She handed it to her father.

Mr. Woodie read it out with a grin. *"To Frieda, the better to look down her nose with."* Bad-tempered Cousin Frieda had thought herself too ladylike to have anything to do with old Sebastian Fall—"That old Gypsy!"—and after fourteen years still called Mrs. Woodie "that awful girl poor Frank married." Mr. Woodie picked at the knot in the string.

"She'll never know," he said. "We'll just tie it up again."

Inside was a pair of gold-rimmed spectacles, the sort with no earpieces, but a slender gold handle on one side instead. It was the kind that rich old ladies in really old movies used. It was called a lorgnette, Tee thought. The rich, old ladies held them up to their eyes, tilted their heads back, and peered down their noses at anybody who wasn't rich enough to suit them. Mr. Witt, who didn't know Cousin Frieda, was the only one who didn't laugh. Some of the other newspaper-wrapped gifts were just as wicked, and almost as funny: the hearing aid for Aunt Stella, whose ears were fine, but who was always too busy talking to listen to anyone else, and the baby pacifiers for Cousin Eddie's noisy six-year-old twins, whose grandfather grumbled that they only stopped screaming when they were eating, or asleep.

"Where's mine?" Tee asked. It was sure to be either a joke, or something as stupid as Charles's, but she was curious anyhow. After all, some of Great-uncle Bass's junky treasures seemed to be valuable, even if they were more weird than nice.

Mr. Woodie, elbow-deep in newspaper, exclaimed, "Hah! I think—yes, here it is." He straightened, bringing up a middling-sized, oblong parcel. "All yours, Princess."

The label said, FOR DEAR LETICIA ANN, MY SHABTI

BOX. Tee read it aloud. "A 'shabti box.' Daddy, what's a shabti box?"

"You've got me, Princess. I never heard the word before."

Mr. Witt shook his head. "Neither have I."

"It's perfectly clear," Charles announced. "It's like 'Chin box,' only 'shab' is for one word, and 'ti' for the other. Shabby tin box? Tie box? Tiara box? Tiddledy-winks box?"

"Oh, shut up," Tee snapped grumpily. To Charles's disgust, she took her time undoing the wrappings, but why be disappointed before you had to be? It certainly wasn't a tiara. She could tell from the longer-than-wider shape. Even before she pulled off the last layer of newspaper, she could tell that it was a box, and probably made of wood.

"Let us see," Charles said eagerly. "Hold it up."

Held up in the flashlight's beam, the box glowed with color: red and white, black, yellow, green and blue. It was about eleven inches tall and five inches square—with longer corner pieces painted to represent columns. The feet of the columns were feet for the box, and their tops were painted to look like palm trees. On three sides, stiff figures of big-eyed women in pleated skirts stood with one leg planted ahead of the other. On the fourth was a woman with a cat's head. A curved lid with a small knob fitted between the column tops.

"Look at that!" Mr. Woodie was surprised. "It's Egyptian. Isn't it?"

Mr. Witt bent close to peer at it. "It's not only Egyptian," he said. "It looks old. *Really* old. It just might be the real thousands-of-years-old McCoy."

Tee gave a scornful sniff. "It looks like a fancy pencil box to me," she said.

Charles was excited. "Open it up, Tee. See what's inside."

"Yes, yes, open it," their father and Mr. Witt echoed.

Tee sniffed again. "It's probably empty." But she wiggled the lid free. A little puff of wood dust rose up to glitter in the dimming beam from the flashlight. "There's *some*thing," she said, and tilted the opening to the light to make sure the something wasn't a spiderweb. "Oh boy, it's a wooden doll," she said flatly as she pulled out a figure rolled in a square of bubbly plastic wrap. "Oh-wow-oh, how great, how dorkish. Exactly what I wanted."

The doll in her hand was the carved figure of a wide-eyed, black-haired girl or young woman. Her stiff, black hairdo was topped by a yellow cap with wings down the sides and a peak at the front like a bird's beak. Her arms were crossed on her chest. From the waist down to her feet she was carved all in one piece, with painted-on white mummy wrappings.

Peculiar squiggles and odd little figures of birds and men were drawn in black ink across the white wrappings in rows. The wide, black-rimmed eyes stared up at Tee like an unblinking cat's.

Mr. Witt rubbed his chin. "She may be a tomb figure, part of some woman's coffin furniture. Buried with her."

"Ee-*yew!*" Tee wrinkled her nose and thrust the figure back into the shabti box. "A *dead* doll."

The flashlight gave one last tremble of light and winked out into pitch darkness.

"Can we go home *now?*" Tee demanded.

THREE

On Tuesday, three weeks and three days later, Tee sat on a bench at the side of the athletic field with other girls in her class. She held her breath. Mrs. Amery's whistle had shrilled, and names began flying through the air the moment the P.E. teacher barked out, "Red and Blue team captains, choose teams—quick time!"

"Robles!"

"Tayler!"

"Purdy!"

"Salvatierra!"

The names shot out, rapid-fire, then slowed as the lineup on the benches dwindled to eight, and then seven. The first week, because Tee was new, the captains chose her fifth or sixth, but by the second week she was down to next-to-next-to-next-to last. If she didn't get called soon—this very minute—she probably would be stuck in the Awkward Squad for good. That was what loud, cheerful Mrs. Amery called the three usual last-chosens, Audra Penny, Anjali Gupta, and Katie Schumacher. Audra, the math whiz, wore thick-lensed glasses and peered through them like a nearsighted mole. Anjali Gupta was the prettiest and probably the nicest girl in school, but the clumsiest, too. Katie could play the piano better than any of the teachers, but she was too timid to kick a dust bunny, let alone a soccer ball.

"Boyce!"

"Simmons!"

"Um—Penny."

Tee's heart sank as Audra fastened on safety glasses and ran out onto the field. Welcome to the Awkward Squad, she told herself. Her cheeks burned.

"Okay—Gupta."

"Tee Woodie, then."

"C'mon, Schumacher, you're a Blue," Mrs. Amery yelled.

At least it was the last period of the day. And not the worst one, Tee thought.

At home, after school, Tee sat at the table that was her bedroom desk and banged her head up and down on her social studies book. If only it could be Friday! If only it were time for Christmas vacation! If only it were next *June* already. June, and not hot.

The shabti box sat forgotten in the closet behind her, at the back of the top shelf. Tee had wanted to give it to the auction-house experts from Phoenix who came to value Great-uncle Bass's treasures. Her parents had been firm. "You can show it to them, but no, you can't sell Uncle Bass's gift. You're going to keep it," they said.

The man and woman from the auction house, when they came, offered to take the entire contents of the treasure room to sell at auction. They told an astonished Mr. Woodie that such a sale might bring well over a hundred thousand dollars. Charles showed them his odd machine. To his delight, it turned out to be a 175-year-old calculator called a De Colmar Arithmometer.

"Sort of a prehistoric computer," Charles had explained happily. Right then and there he decided to switch from collecting beetles to collecting calculators.

"Besides," he said, "there are just too many kinds of beetles. Did you know there are five thousand kinds of *cockroaches?* I would've liked to have a Hissing Cockroach from Madagascar, but the dead ones can't hiss. This is better."

Tee was determined to dislike the shabti and its box, and decided at the last minute to return it to her closet without showing it to the experts. If she couldn't sell it, knowing that it was worth a hundred dollars or so would be like having a fancy box of fudge you weren't allowed to eat. Better not to know.

That was weeks ago, soon after school started, and Tee was every bit as miserable at Oasis Wells Middle School as she had feared. First, she had found herself sentenced to beady-eyed Mrs. Chatto's homeroom. Worse than that, Charles had been allowed to skip a year—for the second time since second grade—so that now he and Tee were in the same grade. He didn't gloat, and he was in a different homeroom and different classes, but it was still humiliating. In the hallway, Tee pretended that she didn't know him. She was dark-eyed and dark-haired, and darker-skinned, and he had their Grandma Smitz's light brown hair and greeny-brown eyes, so ignoring him worked, but only for a week or two. Then everyone caught on. To make Tee even more bad-tempered, Charles, in spite of being a new student and class peewee, was elected to the student council. Tee decided that she was cursed. She had Mrs. Raymond, better known as "the Spider Woman," for math. Mrs. Raymond dressed all in black and was almost skeleton-thin, but the nickname came because of her way of gliding up behind and pouncing on students who doodled on their papers or wrote down wrong answers. "HAH!" she said, and tapped a long, purple fingernail on the guilty paper. At least once every math class, it seemed, her unexpected "HAH!" sounded in Tee's ear. Having nice, good-looking Mr. Duran for history wasn't any better. Every single time he asked her a question in class—every single time—she gave the wrong answer or had to say, "I don't know." It was a curse. So was Mr. Duran's homework assignment for Thursday.

Tee lifted her head to stare at the sheet of paper. "*(1) Read Chapters 5 through 7*," it read. She had done that, but the only fact that stuck in her head was that Ancient Egypt had lasted for five thousand years. Part (2) was "*Write a half-page report <u>in your own words</u> to answer <u>and to explain</u> one of the following questions:*

(a) Why did the ancient Egyptians want the river Nile to flood every year?
(b) What are hieroglyphics?
(c) Did the Egyptians worship many gods, or just one?
(d) Were all of the pharaohs of Egypt Egyptians?"

A whole half page? She looked at what she had written: "*The ancient Egyptians wanted the Nile River to flood so that they could grow crops on the riverbanks.*" What else was there to say? That was *it*. Period.

She chewed on her pencil for a while and then began again on a new sheet of paper. "*The ancient Egyptians lived in ancient Egypt, where it hardly ever rained. They wanted the Nile River to flood up over the riverbanks so that they could plant their crops on the riverbanks that were flooded.*" It was longer, but still was nowhere near half a page. Even if she stretched out her handwriting, it wouldn't be close.

A knock at the door made her jump. Charles stuck his head in without waiting for an answer. "Tee? Can you help with my history report?"

Tee dropped her pencil in surprise, and bent to pick it up. Charles? Asking for help? She straightened and shrugged, hiding her pleasure. "Sure, I guess."

"I've decided to write about hieroglyphics," Charles announced as if it were the News of the Day. He pushed his glasses back up the bridge of his nose. "I found a whole book on the Egyptian language in Great-uncle Bass's library, but I need some hieroglyphics to look up in it. Can I borrow the doll in your Shabby Tiddledywinks box?"

"Oh." Tee's cheeks turned pink. She might have known he wouldn't be asking for *help*-help. "I guess so. It's up on the closet shelf. Behind the shoe boxes with my china shoes." The little china shoes were a collection Grandma Smitz had started for her and added to every birthday and Christmas. Tee secretly liked them even though they were so "girlie" that they crossed the line into dorky. She only put them out when Grandma came to visit.

"Are you going to take it in to class?" she asked Charles in a nastily sugary voice. "That's so *sweet*. Just like first-grade show-and-tell. But what if the writing only says something dumb like, 'I'm Dolly and I belong to Whosis, and we live at Number Two Pyramid Street?' Bo-ring."

Charles shrugged. "I'd make it into a joke, then. It'd still tell how hieroglyphics work." He hesitated. "Maybe I'll just copy them down. I don't need to take the box and the doll to class." He leaned over to look at her paper. "Um—can I use your other chair for a step stool?"

"Oh, go ahead," Tee grumbled. "Get the silly box, and let me finish *my* report."

Charles's glasses slipped down again as he straightened. "You could say *why* they couldn't grow stuff on the riverbanks unless they had a flood every year," he suggested. He dragged the chair into the closet and climbed up onto it. "You could say what they grew. And you could tell about the canals for irrigation and all that. That's in Great-uncle Bass's old encyclopedia."

"I know. I was going to. I only just started, Mister Know-It-All." Tee snatched the chair back after he jumped down with the painted box, and followed to bang the door shut behind him.

"I was going to," she grumbled as she sat down and turned back to the beginning of Chapter Five.

After school on Wednesday, Tee walked the three blocks to the County Public Library. At a little after five o'clock she checked out three creepy-sounding titles, then walked the block and a half to Look and Listen! to catch a ride home with her father when the shop closed. At home, she headed straight for her room, sat down at the table, and tried again to think about the river Nile. She chewed on her pencil. Thinking was hard with *The Ghost and Ginger Nye* and *Jessica Jackson and the Ruby Mirror of Rahjastan* and *The World Under the Windy Mountains*, beaming, "Readme!readme!readme!" messages from her backpack. The temptation was hard to resist, but her Nile paragraph was due tomorrow, and she had math and English homework, too. She put in a bit about the farmers growing grain, and flax for making linen, on the riverbanks. What were the other things Charles told her to put in? He had named two things, and she needed just two more sentences—if she rewrote the paragraph and slanted her writing far enough sideways. Two more sentences ought to bring it right to the middle of the page.

An hour later, Charles bounced back in with the shabti box. He flapped some papers at Tee. "Tee-sha? Here's your dolly back, and I found them all!"

"All what?" She slipped *The Ghost and Ginger Nye* under her social studies book as she straightened.

"All the hieroglyphs. What else? Some are like pictures that mean words, but the others are sounds. Sort of an alphabet without any real vowels, but there are sounds like"—he looked at the first paper—"like *yeh* and *wd* or whatever. I'll read you what I think the writing on the doll says, okay?"

"*No*," Tee said. "I'm trying to work. Just put the stupid box back and go away."

"No, look, it's really cool writing." Charles spread the paper out in front of her and pushed his glasses up his nose. "Look. These are all signs that stand for letters. These letters right below are what the writing on your shabti says."

Tee sighed and barely glanced at the alphabet sheet. On the second sheet, what she saw was:

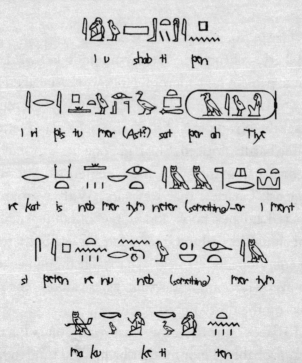

"See," Charles said. "I've put the sounds they stand for on the lines in between. Like, the little chick is *W*. The straight feather-thing is *yeh*, and the leg, that's *B*. So the whole label on the doll is—" Charles read slowly, in the closest he could come to a deep, eerie movie-mummy voice.

> *"Ee-oo shabti pen*
> *irry pistoo mer Ast sat perah Tiye*
> *rekkat is neb mertim netter* something-*er iment,*
> *si petten renoo neb* something *mertim*
> *makoo ketty ten."*

"Great. So, what does it *mean?*"

Charles shrugged. "How should I know? I only have to explain how hieroglyphics work to make *Egyptian* words. I don't need to look them up in English." He set the box on top of the bookshelves, and left.

Tee hardly noticed. She had gone back to staring at her own paragraph. Two more sentences. She would never ask Charles, that was sure. With a groan, she gathered up her book and notebook and pencil and went along the hall to Great-uncle Bass's library to find the encyclopedia. Unless Charles had highjacked it into his own room, it was somewhere among the dusty books on the dusty library shelves.

To Tee's surprise, the dust was gone. Charles's work, probably. Their mother hadn't had time to tackle the library. The house was so large, and Great-uncle Bass had fired his housekeeper months before he died, so there was a lot to clean. Disgustingly perfect Charles could be a mega-pain in the behind, but every once in a while he was useful.

The family's new computer was set up on the long table, and the volumes of Great-uncle Bass's old *Blackett's Encyclopedia* stood beside it in their own low bookcase on wheels. Tee was wading through the small print of the encyclopedia entry under *"Nile, River"* when her father's call rang up from the front hall. "Princess? Tee? Your mother says to remind you you're the kitchen helper today. Time to come down and set the table!"

"Coming!" Tee called absentmindedly. At what sounded like a mumbled echo of her answer, she looked up, startled. "Coming," she called again, and listened, but heard nothing. She shrugged, and started reading again from *"The inundation brought rich, black silt,"* where her finger marked the place. On a piece of scrap paper she wrote down *"rich, black silt"* and *"irrigation channels,"* enough to give her two or three more sentences. When she returned the M-O volume to its bookcase, her hand hesitated for a moment over the S-T-U volume and then pulled it out. Not that she really cared (she told herself), but since she was there and the encyclopedia was there, she might as well look up the word *shabti*.

The short entry under *Shabti* read:

The shabti (or shawabti or ushabti) is a half-mummy figure of wood, stone, or faience, usually five to eight inches tall, that was placed in a tomb to accompany and serve the deceased into the Afterlife. The custom of providing a shabti for the pharaoh originated during the period of the Middle Kingdom, and in later times they came to be used in the tombs of nobles and commoners. In life, even the nobles and the wealthy were required by Pharaoh to contribute their labor to such projects as plowing the fields or maintaining the irrigation systems, and they sent servants in their places. It was expected that the same sort of labor would be needed in the Afterlife. Some shabtis are shown holding the tools for specific jobs; others may have been meant as all-purpose substitutes for their masters or mistresses. The shabti spell, written either on the shabti or the coffin, when spoken, orders the magical figure to perform the labors as required.

The next thing Tee knew, the old dinner gong that hung in the front hallway went *bong-bong-bong!* She jumped up in alarm. The table—she hadn't set the table! Flinging the door open into the hallway, she raced out and down the wide stairs. If there wasn't time even to get the napkins out—well, her mother never got angry, only disappointed, but somehow that was worse.

Tee dashed through the old-fashioned double-wide doorway to the dining room, and saw to her surprise that the table was set already. Her father was filling the water glasses. Her mother came in from the kitchen with a steaming baking dish of what looked like lasagna, to set it down on the brass trivet beside her place. Charles—surprise, surprise—was already seated, and rearranging his knife and spoon.

Mrs. Woodie reached for a serving spoon. "Thanks for setting the table, Tee, honey, even if you did forget the forks. I like the flowers, and it's nice to use Great-uncle's good silverware once in a while."

Tee stared, baffled, first at her mother, and then at the table.

A knife and spoon lay crosswise on each plate. A spray of white yarrow and a small cluster of pink spider flowers from the long-neglected garden lay on each side. More blossoms floated in a bowl in the middle of the table. Tee slid a suspicious look at Charles first, and then at her father, but both wore innocent smiles.

"I'll—I'll get the forks," Tee said. She wondered which of them had played Good Fairy. The forks, when she found them, were still badly tarnished, but no one seemed to mind. The lasagna was so good, though, and the apple pie that followed it, that she forgot to ask who really had done her job.

She forgot about more than that. She was in her bedroom, erasing her third try at solving the nastiest of the math problems the Spider Woman had assigned, when her mother's call floated up the stairs. "Tee? Haven't you forgotten the other half of your job? These dishes aren't going to wash and dry themselves."

Tee sighed, closed her eyes, and dropped her forehead onto the math book. Raising it again, she groaned out loudly, "I'm co-o-oming!"

In the same instant, behind her, a strange, distant voice said, *"Maku keti ten."*

Tee froze, then snapped, "Charles, you cut that out!" She turned.

No one was there.

No one was there, and the bedroom door was closed. When she snatched it open to look out, the upstairs hall was empty. The old house was not cold, but Tee shivered. It was the house, she told herself. Anyone would start imagining things in a big old stone house with corner turrets like a castle, and creaking floors and spiders spinning new webs as fast as you knocked the old ones down, and with two-or-three-hundred-year-old paintings of beady-eyed people as spooky as ghosts watching you from dark corners. Charles wasn't in his room. His books and schoolwork were already packed neatly into his backpack ready for tomorrow, so he was probably downstairs watching

Mastermind, or something even brainier, with their parents. Tee had five math problems left to do, but even dishwashing sounded better than being upstairs alone. She pushed the question sheet away and went down.

From the hallway, Tee took a quick look through the living room's open double doors. Three heads were silhouetted above the back of the sofa and an armchair. The television flickered and chattered away. Tee headed down the hall toward the kitchen door behind the stairs, but stopped with her hand on the door. The *clink-clink* of silverware, the *tink-tink* of glasses, and the clatter of dishes sounded busily on the other side.

If her mother was washing up the dishes, who was the third person in the living room? Tee opened the door a crack and peered through it.

The figure standing at the sink with her back to Tee was a stranger. Her movements were oddly jerky, so that the plates and glasses clinked and clattered against each other. She was dressed in a short-sleeved white midriff blouse and a long, pleated white skirt, and she wore leather sandals, and bracelets of bright beads on her upper arms. A cap shaped like a golden bird with bright wings covered the top of a mass of black hair so big that it looked like a wig.

A small square of bubbled plastic wrap was stuck to the back of her skirt.

FOUR

Whoever-it-was stacked the dishes to one side as she dried them. Tee inched the door a little further open, but all she could see was the back and arms, and the hands picking up and drying and putting down. Tee closed the kitchen door silently, and stood frozen, eyes shut. She had not seen what she had just seen. Of course she hadn't. She couldn't have. An *opti-whatsis*, that was what it was. An *optical illusion*? That wasn't the right word for an illusion that was more in your head than in your eyes, though. *Hallucination*? That was it.

The shabti box and all the reading about the river Nile had put Egyptians into her head. She hadn't seen her mother's face when she looked into the living room, only the back of a head. The third person must be a visitor. It had to be her mother in the kitchen. A visitor wouldn't be doing the dishes, and certainly not some crazy-lady visitor in an Egyptian costume. But then, her mother wasn't dressed like that, either. The costume was all her own invention. Or a mirage.

Tee opened her eyes and found herself still standing with her hand on the doorknob. Turning it, she eased the door open a crack, but there was nothing to see. The kitchen was dark. More confused than ever, Tee snatched her hand away, but then pushed the door wide open. She groped around on the near wall for the light switch and flicked it on.

The dishes and pans were stacked neatly to one side of the sink. The cutlery was lined up in a row on the counter on the other side. Whoever the dishwasher had been, she had gone out through the door into the dining room. In a daze, Tee shoved everything into the cupboard or drawer where it belonged, switched off the light, and went out to the living room.

"That was fast," Mrs. Woodie observed as Tee plumped down in the squooshy armchair. The chair had been vacuumed a dozen times since the family moved in, but still sneezed out dust when anyone sat on it.

Tee sat very still and stared at her mother in alarm.

"Phew!" Mr. Woodie flapped a hand in front of his nose. "Glad to have you with us for a change, Princess, but we're going to have to get rid of that chair if we don't all remember not to sit down like a ton of rocks."

"Are you all right, Tee?" her mother asked. "Why are you hugging your stomach?"

"Am I? Oh," Tee said vaguely. "Maybe—maybe I had too much fudge sauce on my ice cream. What are we watching?" She squirmed around to face the TV set. It was a rerun of a *National Geographic* special on animals and language. Grumpily, Tee wondered why on earth anyone would care whether animals or birds could understand words.

"Daddy?" she asked suddenly. "Who was here before I came down? I thought I heard somebody."

"No, nobody here but us chickens," he answered absently.

Tee fidgeted around in the big chair. Had she imagined the whole thing, mysterious dishwasher and all? The dishes *had* been washed. Her stomach did feel a little queasy. She put her hand over her heart. It was going *thumpeta-thump*. She felt her forehead, and it was warm. Maybe she was coming down with the flu. What if everything had been an hallucination, and the dishes were still dirty in the sink? Or—then, what if the neat stacks of dishes had really been dirty, and she had been so befuddled that she put them straight into the cupboard, and the dirty knives and forks and spoons in the dining room sideboard's cutlery drawer? She would have to look to make sure. She *hated* Great-uncle Bass's house. Now even the kitchen was creepy!

Unwillingly, Tee pushed herself up out of the over-stuffed chair. "I think I'll get a drink of water," she mumbled.

"Are you *sure* you're all right?" Mrs. Woodie called, keeping her eyes on the TV. "There's a bottle of fizzy water in the fridge. That might help settle your stomach. I hope it's only indigestion. I don't think there's any flu around yet."

"I'm all *right*," Tee answered grumpily from the hall.

The kitchen was as tidy as she thought she had left it. The dishes in the cupboard were clean—almost. Several of the glasses and dinner plates still wore faint smudges of grease. So did the blades of the dinner knives and the bowls of one or two spoons. Tee snatched a paper towel from the roller and began to rub away furiously at the worst bits. The only person in the family who left smears was Tee herself. Her mother and father and Charles used really hot water and a scrub brush, and left everything sparkling. Tee was always in too much of a hurry to finish to be that picky. At a burst of laughter from down the hall in the living room, she began to be angry.

"I *didn't* wash them!" she said under her breath with a stamp of her foot. "And I'm not going to wash them all over again." If someone was pulling a fancy practical joke, it wasn't funny. She threw the paper towels in the kitchen bin, slammed out through the swinging door,

41

and strode back to the living room to throw herself down again in the fat armchair.

"*Tee!*" her father protested. He covered his nose with a hand as the dust flew. "Do we have to get you a hearing aid?" He flapped at the dust with a magazine. "Phew! That does it. Tomorrow that thing goes to the dump."

Charles hadn't moved from the other chair, and he didn't look as if he was holding back giggles. His eyes were glued to the TV screen.

Tee wasn't sure why, but slamming the door and raising an explosion of dust had made her feel much better. She glared at the TV so hard that for a flicker of a moment she went cross-eyed and saw two talking parrots. Settling down, she tried hard to concentrate on the screen. By the time the gorilla began to talk in sign language, she was so interested that she forgot about the phantom dishwasher. For a while, at least.

When the show was over and Mr. Woodie had switched the TV off, Charles headed upstairs with Tee trailing behind. It was already a little past their 9:30 school-night bedtime. Tee resented that since Charles was in the same grade at school, he had graduated to the 9:30 Lights Out, too. Having to go to bed at the same time as your little brother was humiliating.

On reaching her room, the first thing Tee did was check the bookshelf where Charles had left the shabti. She felt silly checking up on a piece of wood, but she looked, anyway. The doll still stood beside its box, and was still nestled in her scrap of plastic wrapping. Tee stuffed it back into its box, dragged her chair into the closet, and returned the box to its place behind the shoe boxes of china shoes. Then, unwillingly, she began to get ready for bed.

By the time she stopped grumbling to herself, she had her pajamas and slippers on. At least Great-uncle Bass's house had two bathrooms, so she didn't have to wait to wash her face and brush her teeth. Charles always took forever, and now, with a bathroom to himself at bedtime, he took a shower almost every night.

Only when Tee was under the covers and reaching out to switch off the bedside lamp did she see the open math book. She had forgotten the five last problems.

"*Urrrrgh!*" She groaned, turned off the lamp, and threw herself back on the pillow. She would finish them before breakfast. Or on the school bus. For once, neither her father nor her mother had remembered to ask whether her homework was finished before they allowed her to watch TV. She giggled. *Always a Good Rule: Never Do Tonight What You Can Put Off Until Tomorrow.* The mystery of the phantom dishwasher forgotten, she wriggled over onto her side and snorted happily into her pillow.

Five minutes later, the door opened. Half asleep, Tee opened one eye and saw her father silhouetted against the hall light. His shadow and the light from the hall spilled across the floor and onto her worktable.

"You asleep?" He glanced at the table and, spying the open book and the pencil lying across a piece of paper, went over to pick up the sheet of math problems. "Don't bother to play possum, Princess. I see that glimmer of eye. These problems—when do you have to turn in the answers?"

"Tomorrow. Second period," Tee muttered.

"Aha. Funny you didn't remember you still had math to do."

"I'll do 'em in the morning," she mumbled into her pillow.

"Good. Then I'll just set your alarm half an hour earlier," he said, and picked the clock up from the bedside table. "There." He crossed back to the worktable to set the clock down beside the math book, out of reach.

"Good night, Princess," he whispered as the door closed behind him. "Pleasant dreams."

"*Grr-rrr!*" Tee punched her pillow into a new shape and buried her face in it.

The dream was more weird than unpleasant.

State Road was paved with yellow bricks all the way from Stonepile Hill down across the highway to River Street. A line of camels laden with treasure chests plodded down it. The road was lined on each side with a row of big, old houses with green trees and front lawns, not one-story stucco houses, palm trees, cactus gardens, and dusty storefronts. Every front lawn wore a sign. One was LOCKS MADE FOR YOUR KEYS. Another, oddly, read, GLADYS AND HENRY HABERDASHERY. There was a house with a sign, BASS'S BOOKSHOP. A door in the house next to it opened, and a small, dark-haired young woman in a long, white skirt glided out, sat down at a table in the middle of the street, and picked up a pencil. She held it awkwardly upright, and wrote slowly. . . .

FIVE

The alarm clock buzzed angrily into Tee's sleep, and she tried to swat the sound away as if it were a bee. After a while it stopped. She burrowed back under the bedclothes, but as soon as she was comfortable, it started up again. She groaned. What morning was it? Thursday? Thursday. *Thursday.* She sat up in a tangle of bedclothes and felt around on the bed table, but found no clock.

Where *was* it? She peered around the room, trying to track down the buzz. Finally she spied the clock on the worktable. What was it doing over there? With a groan she climbed out of bed and stumbled over to smack down the alarm button on top. The clock read 6:30. *Six-thirty?* Then she remembered. Her father had reset the alarm to get her up in time to finish her math. Her stupid math problems. She groaned. What she wanted to do was to fall back into bed and pull the covers over her head. She might have done just that if her eye hadn't been caught by the colorful math book cover, with its pattern of blue and orange and yellow everyday numbers, and Roman numerals, and Chinese, and two or three other kinds. Sticking out from under the book was the sheet of math problems.

The five unfinished problems had been worked out. Their answers were neatly underlined.

Tee rubbed her eyes, bewildered, and bent down for a closer look. No mistake. Her math homework was finished, like magic. Neither of her parents would have done it. And Charles? No way. But the weirdest thing? The weirdest thing was that the shapes of the numbers looked—almost—like her own handwriting. From close up, they seemed faintly wrong. The lines were trembly, as if the strokes had been written slowly, with the pencil held straight up, here and there making little snags in the paper. With the pencil straight up . . .

Tee shivered and took a step backward. She hugged her arms to her chest. "But I dreamed that, didn't I?" she whispered. *Hadn't* she? Without taking her eyes off the paper, she backed away until she came up against the bed. She sat down, still hugging herself.

Bit by bit, she dredged up scraps of the dream—for parts of it *had* been only a dream. It was the bit after the camels that worried her. There had been a dark young woman in a long white sundress and really big hair. Or was it a wig? There had been a shiny little something hanging in her hair, too. Tee decided uneasily that she must have invented her out of the split-second shape she imagined she saw in the kitchen. Kitchen-Big-Hair and Dream-Big-Hair wore the same sundress, armlets, and hairdo, and had the same stubby fingers as the wooden doll on the closet shelf. That was one of the ways dreams worked, wasn't it? They picked up scraps of things that didn't make sense and stitched them into stories.

Tee stared, unseeing, at the closet door and the bookshelves beside it as she tried to remember what had happened next. Big Hair had come out—she had come out of a house next door to a . . . a bookstore. That was it: a bookstore. Tee had seen Big Hair writing—of that she was sure. The memory of where she sat and what she was writing was floating around somewhere in her head but kept slipping away, like a bead of mercury from a finger that tries to touch it. The only thing that came to her was that Big Hair had been writing with a pencil, holding it straight up. Tee bit her lip. *A straight-up pencil. In short, stubby fingers.*

Tee took a deep breath.

There were two possible explanations. Possibility Number One: She had sleepwalked to the table and finished the math assignment herself. Possibility Number Two: She had half wakened from a dream, seen Big

Hair working out the problems—*really*—and then slid back into sleep to weave it all into her dream.

Tee's eyes widened. *The closet door.* It was next to the bookshelves. Was that what the door and bookstore meant? That the doll came out of the door next to the bookshelves? Tee shivered. Just because a dream might make itself out of echoes from the real world didn't mean that any of it was true or made even a crumb of sense. Still . . .

The words from the encyclopedia echoed in her head: "*. . . the shabti spell orders the magical figure to perform the labors required . . .*"

Tee sat on the edge of her bed and stared at the closet door. It was seven-fifteen and time to get dressed, but she was almost afraid to move. Any second, her father would call, "Breakfast in five minutes!" Drawing a deep breath, she straightened her back and, speaking gruffly, imitated him.

"Ten past seven, Princess. Get dressed! You have five minutes to get dressed before breakfast. You don't want to miss the school bus."

She was opening her mouth to answer in her own voice, "Oh, yes, I do," when the closet door opened.

The shabti stood in the doorway, and it was as tall as she was. It stepped forward, crossed its hands on its breast, and bowed low.

"*Maku keti ten, sat perah Tiye,*" it said.

Tee stared, goggle-eyed, as the strange figure whisked back into the closet with a swirl of its pleated skirt. It was as tall as Tee, but was not at all—real. Its skin was golden-brown, the flat eyes large and black and heavily made-up, its long, squared-off hairdo a heavy mass of tiny braids, its fingers stubby, and its movements quick and jerky. The pleats of the linen skirt were as sharp and narrow as if they had been cut by a knife. The gold beads of the bracelets looked flat, more painted than real.

Almost at once, the shabti reappeared with clothing over one arm and a pair of Tee's summer sandals in the other hand. It bowed again, laid the clothes out neatly on the bed and, before Tee realized what was happening, began to peel off her pajama top. Tee was too astonished—and too frightened—to pull away. The pajama bottoms followed the top. In less than a minute Tee found herself dressed in the long, crinkle-pleated skirt from her old Halloween gypsy costume, and a thermal mesh undershirt. The sandals were fastened on her feet. The stubby fingers whizzed and fluttered through her hair. Tee's fake teardrop-pearl necklace was fastened around her head with the pearl in the middle of her forehead.

The shabti bowed again, and vanished.

Tee looked down at herself and then at the closet door in disbelief. She was too numb with surprise to decide whether she wanted to laugh or scream. She decided she was more terrified than anything else, but under the fear she felt a first tiny fizz of excitement.

"Tee? Breakfast!" her father called.

That broke the spell. Without thinking, Tee dashed to the closet to snatch out a blouse and sweater and her school-uniform skirt. One quick look at her costume in the mirror on the inside of the closet door showed her a laughable version of the shabti itself. She did like the hairdo, though. Her thick hair, partly done in tiny braids, was gathered off to one side with the rest into a neat, fat ponytail. She sped to the chest of drawers for socks and underwear, rescued her shoes from under the worktable, bundled everything together, and ran for the bathroom.

Charles, of course, was always at the breakfast table, washed, toothbrushed, and dressed, before he had to be called. Not until Tee had raced halfway through her honey cornflakes did she realize that she had gone into the terrifying closet that the—the Egyptian—had come out of. It had been her perfectly ordinary, untidy, completely unmagical closet. Numbly, she pinched herself and decided that, yes, she was awake.

Afterward, Tee could not remember eating breakfast, or her mother's compliment on her hair, or leaving the house. She did remember the wait at the bus stop. That was when she asked Charles whether he had found out what any of the ancient Egyptian words spelled out by the hieroglyphics meant in English.

Charles nodded. "I decided you were right and that everybody else'd be interested, too, so I posted a question about the whole writing on a couple of Egyptian archaeology bulletin boards on the Internet."

Tee rolled her eyes up in boredom as Charles chattered on. He would get to the point sooner or later. Trying to hurry him never worked.

"It's lucky I did," Charles said earnestly. "Three people put up answers to tell me that only bits of what I figured out made sense. They told me some really cool stuff, though, like if the little people and birds and stuff are facing left, you read from left to right, like we do. If they're facing right, you read everything from right to left. Anyhow, they said they couldn't help unless they could see the real thing, but we don't have hieroglyphics on our computer, so—"

The State Road bus came in sight, and Tee groaned. The bubble of excitement deep down inside her was beginning to make her stomach ache. They would be at school before he got to the point.

Charles gave her one of his patient wise-old-man looks. "Okay, okay. Anyhow, one of them gave me the e-mail address for a professor at London University, and *he* said if I faxed him the hieroglyphs, he'd e-mail me what it means. So I did, on Mom's fax machine, and this morning he did. I'll copy the English one out for you if you want me to."

"Yes, *please!*" Tee gasped as the bus door wheezed open.

Charles gave her a my-sister-Miss-Potato-Head look that made her want to smack him. But not with the bus driver and half a dozen grown-up passengers for witnesses.

Charles made his way toward the back of the bus, but Tee plumped down in the first empty seat. Beside her, Katie Schumacher tucked her skirt closer to make room, and smiled shyly. "Hi, Tee."

"Oh, hi," Tee answered absently. Turning, she craned to see back down the aisle, but could see only a bit of the top of Charles's head behind the two taller boys in the seat in front of him. Exactly *when* was he going to write out what the writing on the doll said? If she had to wait until after school, she'd be pulling out her hair. Three or four times, Katie looked as if she might be about to say something. Each time she was defeated when Tee turned to scowl back in Charles's direction. At last, when the bus was only half a block from school, a folded-up sheet of lined yellow paper came bobbing up from the back.

In a moment all of the children were up and clutching backpacks and pushing forward. Tee let Katie out, waited until everyone else was past, and got out last, reading as she went. Scowling at Charles's squiggly handwriting, she trailed up the sidewalk and into the school building.

> *"Tee—enciclopedia says shabtis are magic figures put in tooms with dead people to be thier servents in the Afterlife. Professer Allerton says yours reads this way—"*

Tee smirked. Charles might be a brain, but he couldn't spell worth spit—and either the encyclopedia or the ancient Egyptians were pretty silly. Live people could use servants. Dead ones couldn't. She read on:

> *"O shabti,*
> *if the Isis, Princess Tiye, is assigned*
> *any work to do there in the Afterlife,*
> *if you are assigned at any time to serve there,*
> *I am here for you, you shall say."*

Princess *Tiye*?

"Oh, wow," Tee whispered. "Oh, double-chocolate-fudge-with-sprinkles wow!"

SIX

If the hieroglyphics were a magic spell . . .

If they *really* were a magic spell . . .

Tee couldn't seem to get past the "if." Her brain spun around in one spot, like a top. When the bell rang to go to math class, Mrs. Chatto stopped her on her way out the door. "Tee, are you all right? You don't look well."

"No, no. I'm all right." Tee ducked through the door. "I'm fine." Following her classmates down the hall, she giggled suddenly and whispered to herself, "Maybe I'm *great*." If the hieroglyphics really were a spell . . .

And if the gibberish Charles had read out loud in her bedroom was close enough to the sound of real ancient Egyptian spell, then—if she wasn't frothing-at-the-mouth-crazy and the shabti really *had* come to life and done the dishes for her . . .

There was the strange table setting, too. She'd almost forgotten that. And its trying to dress her.

"Tee Woodie, can you tell us whether Jason's answer is the right one?"

Tee looked around and found that she had come into math class, sat down, and opened her book. She hadn't heard a word since class started, and she didn't know what the question was.

"HAH!" The Spider Woman's long, purple fingernail tapped sharply on Tee's math book. Tee jumped.

Mrs. Raymond—the Spider Woman—folded her arms and tapped her foot. "Tee, I see that the answer to problem seven on your paper is different from Jason's answer. Which answer is correct?"

Tee blinked at what Jason had written on the blackboard, but then realized that—if the shabti spell was real—she was safe, whatever Jason's answer was. "Mine?" she looked up at the Spider Woman doubtfully.

"That's right." Ms. Raymond nodded. "Now, can you tell us what you did differently from Jason to get your answer?"

Tee flushed. "Uh, I forget."

The day went downhill from there, but in between disasters, Tee's mind danced around in a wider and wider circle. Say that the gibberish Charles had read out loud in her bedroom was the real ancient Egyptian spell. Say that a magical shabti heard it and woke up. If it did wake up, wouldn't it have to think *this* was the Afterlife? *And* if it had been buried thousands of years ago with a dead princess named Tiye, then—then it must have heard her name Tee as "Tiye." It must have heard her father call her "Princess," and tell her to set the table. That would be why it had set the table, and done the dishes and her homework, and tried to dress her.

"Because it thinks it's my *magic shabti now!"*

Her eyes sparkled, and she bounced up and down a little on the balls of her feet.

"All right, Tee," Mrs. Avery yelled. "If you're that full of beans, what are you waiting for? You're It!"

"What?" Tee yelped, startled. Then she remembered that she was on the playground, gym period had started, she was holding the ball, and standing behind the volleyball net. The rest of the girls were watching, some giggling, and the rest trying not to. Audra Penny gave her a shove toward the back. "It's your serve."

Tee made four good serves in the next half hour, and no one looked more surprised each time than Tee herself. Mrs. Amery was startled at last into a loud, "Well done!"

Tee was relieved when the game was over. She had more important things to think about.

In the school bus on the ride home, Tee struggled to write in her notebook in spite of the jiggles and bumps from the bus's bouncy springs and every bump, crack, and pothole on the way. Audra Penny, following her down the aisle and plumping down in the seat beside her, was another bump. Her thick glasses gave her a peering, curious look, so Tee held the front cover of the notebook on her lap straight up and her head down to hide what she wrote. At the end of the twenty-minute ride, she had:

> S. understands English (or no table or dishes
>   or dressing) How? It only talked old Egyptian.
> What did the old Es think life would be like
>   when they were living in the Afterworld after
>   they were dead?
> Why doesn't it know my bedroom isn't in that
>   place?

At home, Charles trailed up the front sidewalk after her. "You were doing homework on the *bus*. Are you sick, or what?" He gave a little skip backward to keep out of range, and when Tee kept going without even a halfhearted "Shut up," he stopped in surprise. Then he shrugged and went on up the porch steps and in to see whether there were still any apples left in the kitchen. Or corn chips. Or both.

Tee went straight up to her room, closed the door, dumped her backpack and the notebook onto her worktable, and dragged the extra chair over to jam its back up under the doorknob. Pulling her desk chair into the closet, she stood on the seat to move the shoe boxes. She hesitated as she reached back for the shabti box. She wasn't sure whether it was because she felt scared or felt silly. Either way, the feeling was like butterflies under her breastbone.

Placing the colorful shabti box on the table, Tee opened it, unwound the square of bubbled plastic wrap, and propped the shabti up against its box. From her backpack, she took her schoolbooks and the school library copy of *Dragon Slayer* and lined them up on the table with a pad of notebook paper, and a pencil. Then she shoved the chair into place, sat down on her bed, and took a deep breath.

"Shabti, write—" The words came out in a squeak, and then a croak. It was only excitement, she told herself. She took another deep breath, squeezed her eyes tight shut, and tried again.

"Shabti, please write a book report on that book, *Dragon Slayer*, for Mrs. Chatto in English class," she said shakily.

When she opened her eyes, the little shabti still stood propped against its box. It stared over Tee's head with its blank, painted gaze. The wide eyes, rimmed with black, like heavy makeup, were only paint, but they gave her a shiver. What if they could see anyway?

If it couldn't understand English, how had it known

to set the table and wash the dishes for her? Tee slid off the bed and turned her back on the shabti to take Charles's note about the hieroglyphics from her pocket and reread it. The charm said, "*. . . if the princess Tiye is assigned.*" Maybe that was it. Maybe it would only do things you *had* to do. Folding up the note, she returned it to her pocket. The shabti had heard her parents tell her to do the math and her kitchen-duty chores, and went and did them, so it *had* to understand English—or at least the thoughts behind the words.

She took a deep breath and tried again. This time she kept her back turned. "I am 'assigned' to write a book report—a—a report about the story in that book—for my English teacher."

She didn't blink, but she didn't see what happened. One moment, the little wooden half-mummy shabti was on the table; in the next, it was standing on the other side of the table, hands together, bowing to her.

"*Maku keti ten,*" it said. The wide, black-rimmed dark eyes fixed on her. They gleamed, but did not blink.

"G-great," Tee stammered. She watched the white-clad figure move away to bend over the table, pencil in hand. Then—*phtt!*—it was gone.

Tee hesitated. The shabti was on the table in exactly the place where she had left it. Tee edged closer and saw that the sheet of notepaper was empty except for a small, neat parade of hieroglyphics across its middle.

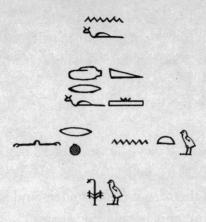

Baffled, Tee stared at the Egyptian characters for several moments before an answer came to her. The magical wooden figure might understand the thoughts behind the words it heard, but it was silly to suppose that it would know how to read English—or write it. Just her luck! She had a magical servant she couldn't use—or didn't know how to use except for rinky-dink chores around the house. That was worse than having a father who owned a video store and wouldn't let her watch video movies on school nights. Worse, even, than having to put Grandpa and Grandma Woodie's birthday and Christmas checks in her savings account every year and never being allowed to spend any of it. Tee stared out across the worktable and over the tops of the cottonwood trees without seeing a thing, and sighed.

She was going to have to do her own homework forever and ever.

SEVEN

After dinner (it was Mr. Woodie's turn to do the dishes) Tee went back to *Dragon Slayer*. It had made a pretty good movie, not as good as *Dragonheart*, but still good. She had watched it on video only two or three weeks ago, and could remember every twist in the plot. All she needed was a quick zip through the book to get the names of the main characters and make sure it had all the same good bits in it.

By the end of the second page, Tee was glad she hadn't sat down to write about the story of the movie without looking. The names *were* all different, for one thing, and the book began with a sea captain telling a story-inside-the-story to a king and his warriors. By the fourth page, it turned out that the sea captain wasn't telling King Hygelac about a dragon at all, but some monster called Grendel. A quick flip through the pages told her that the dragon didn't even appear until almost the end, and that *Dragon Slayer*–the-book and *Dragon-slayer*–the-movie had nothing at all to do with each other. She slammed the book shut in disgust.

"Grr-*rrh!*"

But she was stuck. She had to read it now. She had left it to the last minute, so she *had* to read it now.

She picked the book up again. "At least you're a skinny one," she grumbled. A hundred and seven pages was a lot better than *Watership Down*, the adventure story about rabbits Charles had picked to write about. Four-hundred-plus pages about rabbits? Tee shuddered. He'd had his nose in it for days.

Reluctantly, Tee settled down with her chin on one hand and *Dragon Slayer* propped up in front of her nose. Mrs. Chatto, like almost every English teacher she ever had, might end up giving her an F for Effort, but Tee, when she wanted to, could read almost as fast as she could slowly turn the pages. Hurrying through adventure stories by flashlight under the bedcovers was good practice. Now she raced through the hero Beowulf's voyage, and the man-eating monster Grendel's attack on King Hrothgar's men. When the story grew gruesome in Beowulf and Grendel's fight, and Beowulf's fight with Grendel's monster-mother in the underwater cave, she slowed down for fear of missing something. As she read, the dusk outside her window grew so deep that finally she found herself peering at the pages with her nose almost touching the book. She switched on the table lamp without taking her eyes from the book. Once the monster's mother was dead, Tee skimmed through the part about Beowulf sailing home and growing old, but slowed down while Beowulf and young Wiglaf fought the dragon, and Beowulf died.

The hero got *killed?* Tee sat still for a moment. At least he was an old man by then. And the dragon didn't get to kill young Wiglaf.

Tee looked at her watch. Twenty minutes to Lights Out. Her parents might be good listeners, and even nicely goofy sometimes, but trying to talk her way around a family rule was a waste of time. It was twenty minutes to Lights Out, and she hadn't written a single word. She couldn't do it in bed. Reading *Jessica Jackson and the Amulet of Debakir* under the covers was easy if you were careful where you pointed the flashlight, but handwriting ended up too squiggly.

She picked up her pencil and glared at the shabti, still propped against its painted box. How could she help it learn English?

She *could* tell Charles everything.

Charles was good at any kind of puzzle. She *could* tell him, but Charles couldn't keep a secret any more than a kitchen strainer could hold water. Besides, right off the bat he would probably shrug and say something obvious like, "Why not just say 'I am required to learn to speak and read and write English better than I do now'?"

Tee blinked. Well, why not say just that? It was true enough, but her own reading and writing wouldn't *get* better just because the shabti learned English. The shabti might figure that out, too. . . .

The answer popped into her head almost as if she had dropped a nickel in an old-fashioned gum-ball machine and had a prize pop out. *Reading. Book. Charles. Charles said Great-uncle Bass had a book about the old Egyptian language.* The book would be in English, and Charles had looked up the English for some words, so it had a glossary. Wouldn't somebody either brainy or magical be able to work it the other way around?

Sixteen minutes.

Tee pushed her chair back so quickly that, if she hadn't already been on her feet, she would have toppled over with it. Leaving it on its back in the middle of the floor, she dashed out and down the hallway to the library. No light showed under Charles's door. The double doofus must still be going to sleep at his old Lights-Out time, half an hour earlier than hers.

In the library, Tee scowled at the bookshelves. It was depressing. They covered all four walls from floor to ceiling except for the two windows and the door. There was a special stepladder for reaching the upper shelves, but she could tell the book she wanted wasn't on the upper shelves. Whoever dusted the room had missed not just the books, but the ladder, and the ladder had no footprints on its dusty treads. She started by skimming along the titles on the shelves at eye level, moving around the room, and back around along the next shelf down—and back around again another shelf lower. Nine minutes.

"It's going to be on the bottom shelf," she muttered to herself. "I know it is." With her luck, if she had started at the bottom, the book would have been at the top.

She found the books about ancient Egypt on the next-to-bottom shelf, and the one she was looking for in between *Royal Tombs* and *From Gizeh to Dongola*. At least, the title was *Egyptian Grammar*, and the top wasn't dusty, like its neighbors'. There was also a *Dictionary of Ancient Egyptian*, and so she took both, snapped off the light, hurried back to her own room, and closed the door behind her.

Six minutes. With *Egyptian Grammar* open on her worktable, Tee took her own dictionary from her bookshelf and set the stage. She opened both dictionaries and propped *Dragon Slayer* open beside them. She switched on the bedside lamp, switched off the overhead light and table lamp, snatched her pajamas from the hook on the back of the closet door, and hurried back out into the hall. From outside her door, she stuck her head back in to speak the speech she had worked out in her head.

"Shabti," she whispered as loudly as she dared. "I am required to know how to read and write English. That's the other language in that big book with Egyptian writing. Then I have to write one whole page that tells about the story in the book on top." She pulled the door closed, then thought for a moment. Opening it again, she added, "In English," and dashed off to the bathroom.

She brushed her teeth. There was no time to take a shower. She looked at the clock as she climbed into her pajamas. One minute! Feeling almost as fearful as eager, she tiptoed to her bedroom with her clothes in one hand and drying her face with the hand towel in the other.

The shabti was propped up against its box, as if it had not moved, but both books were closed. The pencil was worn down. The sheet of notepaper was full. The title at the top read, *"The Story of the Dragon Slayer,"* and the first sentence began, *"This is the story of a strange time and a strange place."* "Wow, great!" Tee crowed. With only seconds to spare, she shut the shabti up in its box, jumped into bed, and turned off the light. Her father, bang on the dot, opened the door and stuck his head in.

"'Night, Princess. All okay?"

"'Night, Daddy. All's great." Tee stretched out happily, but then put her pillow over her face for fear he could see her grin in the dark.

EIGHT

Tee's head was so a-whirl with excitement and ideas that it was a long time before she fell asleep. In the morning, her alarm rang at a quarter to seven, as usual. She rose, rubbed the sleep from her eyes, and was in the bathroom, blinking at herself in the mirror with her mouth full of toothpaste, before she remembered.

"By Bagical Boop Breport!" She flashed herself a frothy grin, rinsed, snatched her towel, and dried her face on the way back to her room.

The neatly written book report still lay on the table. She hadn't imagined it. But now, as she tried to skim down the neat lines while she pulled on her socks and then stepped into her skirt, she saw what she hadn't thought of at bedtime: It was printed, not written in longhand. Mrs. Chatto would have a fit. On the first day of class she had warned, "Printing is for little children and computers. You're too grown-up for printing, so all the homework you do for me will be in longhand. If you print, you will have to redo it and you'll be marked down a full grade." She had stuck to that rule, too, even with left-handed Tony Hackman, whose joined-up writing was so tilted and scrunched together that she must go cross-eyed trying to read it.

Tee scrambled into her sweater and shoes and sat down to copy out the report in longhand. After five lines, she could see that there was no way it would all fit on one page, and no way she could finish before ten to eight, when the school bus came. There were a lot of weird bits, too, like *"He huge and horrible"* instead of "He *was* huge and horrible," or *"then thanked they him"* instead of "then they thanked him." These slowed her down even more, so she made up for it by leaving some of them out.

"Tee! Where are you? Come and eat your breakfast, or you'll be late for the bus!" her mother called from downstairs.

Tee jammed her books into the book bag, snatched up the notebook and pencil, and raced downstairs. As soon as she had gulped down her orange juice and cereal, she began scribbling at top speed where she left off.

Charles wiped his mouth with his napkin, missing most of his milk mustache, and pushed his chair back. He shrugged on his backpack and came to look over her shoulder on his way to the door. "Why're you copying that all out again?"

Tee wrote on. "It's for Mrs. Chatto. I forgot last night that she takes off a grade if it's printed." She decided not to tell him about his mustache.

"Thirteen till," Mrs. Woodie called from the kitchen. Tee scooped up her paper and notebook and hurried after Charles.

On the bus, she tried hard to keep her writing as even as before, but it was hard to keep the squiggles out. The morning chatter around her was as loud as ever, and she had to sit half sideways so that she couldn't see mousy little Katie Schumacher beside her. Tee didn't want her to see, and think that she was copying someone else's homework. Well, she was but she wasn't.

At school, she copied out another paragraph before the late bell. She finished the last sentence between Mrs. Chatto's first-period "Good morning, class," and her "Will the monitors please collect the book reports?" As Tee's paper made its way up to Mrs. Chatto's desk, she gave a sigh of relief and happily forgot about it until after the surprise spelling test. That was when Mrs. Chatto called on Anjali Gupta to read her book report. Tee, sitting near the back of the room, didn't hear a word of it after "This is really an exciting adventure." Her eyes were on the wall clock: four— three long minutes to go before the bell.

"Tee Woodie? Will you come up, Tee?" Mrs. Chatto watched over the gold rims of her glasses as Tee took her time getting up, and took the long way around the desks to the front of the room.

"Tee surprised me," Mrs. Chatto said. "She chose Rosemary Sutcliff's *Dragon Slayer*, a retelling of a story that's over a thousand years old. Tee, tell us why you chose—"

The bell rang just as Tee opened her mouth. Saved by the bell!

Mrs. Chatto made a sign to Tee to stay where she was while the rest of the class filed out on their way to Mr. Duran's room. "Why *did* you choose *Dragon Slayer*?"

Tee flushed. "I thought it was the book of the movie *Dragonslayer*," she answered sheepishly. "I didn't find out till it was too late to pick another one."

Mrs. Chatto almost laughed, but turned it into a hiccup and a smile. "Well, that's honest. Um, it's a good report, Tee, but it would be better still if it didn't sound a bit too much like a dictionary. Next time try to use words that sound more like Tee Woodie. Off you go now. You don't want to be late."

"Yes! Yes! Yes!" Tee whispered to herself as she half walked, half ran to Mr. Duran's room at the far end of the hall. She was going to have to learn how to use the shabti, but it did *work*. Except for the "sounding like a dictionary"

part. She would have liked to ask what was wrong with sounding like a dictionary, anyway? The English workbook and Mrs. Chatto herself went on about learning at least ten new words a day. Still, the bell had rung just in time. What if Mrs. Chatto had time to ask what one of the shabti's fancy words, like *quietus* or *affright*, meant?

As Tee scuttled into her seat in Mr. Duran's social studies class, a sudden thought brought her down to earth. What did "like Tee Woodie" mean? There was no way Mrs. Chatto could suspect that she hadn't written the report, was there? Tee opened *Our World* and settled down uneasily to watch Mr. Duran write on the blackboard *For Monday: Read Chapter 8, on Ancient Rome*. Her hand shot up.

"Yes, Tee? What is it?"

"Are we finishing the ancient Egyptians today, then?" Tee asked anxiously.

"Yes." Mr. Duran looked surprised and a little mystified. "That's what we said yesterday, Tee. Why do you ask?"

"No reason," Tee mumbled. Disappointed, she scooted down a little in her seat as she copied the assignment for Monday. If she had known about the shabti a week ago, it could have done all of the Egyptian homework standing on its head. Even made a model of the Nile Valley. Then she cheered up. It would just have to learn about the Romans. Maybe she would volunteer to make a model of whatever that stadium was where the Romans held their chariot races. With half an ear tuned to Mr. Duran's first question and Audra Penny's answer, she began to make a list in tiny handwriting at the bottom of her notebook page:

TO DO TOMORROW at library
Return bks.
Get books.

GET AT VID. SHOP
The Mummy
Arabian Nights
a *Batman*
The Princess Bride
Ever After
the new *Sinbad*

Her parents allowed her only three videos a week, but Ginny, the afternoon salesclerk, never bothered to check anything except that they were rated okay for kids. She could get away with six if her father wasn't at the front counter, and as long as she got out of bed early enough on Saturday and Sunday morning to watch the extra two before anyone else was up. The *Batman* would be for Charles, so he wouldn't rat on her.

The weekend was perfect, except for one or two small, familiar miseries. On Friday evening the Woodies went out to dinner at Ristorante Polacco, where the chicken risotto turned out to be both tasteless and gloppy. Afterward they drove back across the river and up to the Palm Tree Mall to look for new shoes for Charles, whose feet were growing faster than the rest of him. Outside the Feet First shop, Anjali Gupta waved as she and Connie Tayler and Angie Beltran from Tee's class passed, arm in arm. Close behind them, two boys from Oasis Wells Middle School called out, "Yo, Charlie! Come to the Ben & Jerry's!" as they raced by. Charles raised his hands helplessly as he turned to follow his father into the shoe shop.

"Go join your friends for an ice cream, Tee," her mother urged. "We'll catch up with you there."

Tee pretended to be looking at the fuzzy bedroom slippers in the window. "They aren't my friends," she said sullenly. "Besides, I'm too full for ice cream."

Mrs. Woodie sighed, and went on into the shop to make sure that Charles did not talk his father into buying another pair of wild sports shoes. What he needed was a pair that wouldn't look silly with his good slacks for church. Tee followed and found a chair off in a corner, where she pulled out the worn school-library copy of *Charlotte Sometimes* and settled down to read.

The rest of the weekend went like a dream, until Sunday evening. Tee moved from one adventure story to another, first solving the mystery of the stolen Golden Eye of Gandahar with Jessica Jackson, getting chased by a stiff-legged mummy in the next story, then swooping and soaring on a magic carpet, being saved from the clutches of Prince Humperdinck, and more. On Saturday afternoon her mother tried, before she left for the shop, to get Tee to call a friend to go swimming "or *some*thing," but, except with her parents and Charles, Tee managed to keep from venturing into the outside world at all.

Late on Sunday afternoon, Tee set out the list of vocabulary words, the ancient Egyptian dictionary and the *Grammar*, and the math workbook, opened to the problems on page thirty-two. She jammed one chair under the doorknob to keep Charles out. She dragged the other into the closet, but instead of climbing up to bring down the painted box from the shelf, she found herself sitting on the edge of her bed. The idea of having a magical servant-in-a-box was as scary as it was exciting. Not knowing how it worked was scary, even if the whole point about magic was that no one *could* know. You just had to take a deep breath and jump in. She made herself get up.

With the box on the table, and her chair back in its place, Tee opened the box and propped the shabti up in front of it. She took a deep breath. *This* time she wouldn't shut her eyes or duck out into the hall. She was going to look straight *at* it.

"Shabti," she announced to the empty room, "my teachers say I have to write good sentences using these words, and answer these questions, and do these math problems."

In a blink, before Tee had finished speaking, the shabti appeared beside the table not four feet away. Tee jumped in alarm.

"*Maku keti ten*. Ee ahm hr'f'ru," it said. It crossed its hands on its breast, as before.

Tee swallowed "First—"

She hesitated, frowning. Something *felt* different about it, but then, she told herself, the only time she had looked straight at it before was when it was just a painted wooden doll. She tried again.

"First, if anyone in this house gives me a job to do, like setting the table and washing the dishes again tonight, wait until they can't see you do it. Nowadays servants are supposed to stay out of sight. Okay?" The fib sounded so snobbish that she blushed as she said it. It was only a stick of wood, and didn't have feelings to hurt, but it was hard to think that a thing that could walk and talk wasn't a person.

The shabti bowed again. "*Yenek beyek k'*. Ee ahm oor sr'ant," it said.

It looked at her blankly, almost as if it waited for an answer. Did it think "Ee ahm oor sr'ant" was English? Tee's eyes widened. Maybe it was. Maybe it was, "I am your servant"?

"S-sure," she said uncertainly. "Thanks."

It wheeled around to sit down stiffly at the table. When it picked up Tee's pencil between thumb and forefinger, this time it was at a slant, not upright. The fingers made the pencil fly across the notepaper. In the blank after the word *Semblance*, they wrote, *"A villain can put on the semblance of goodness."*

Tee blinked, but decided that by now Mrs. Chatto probably didn't expect her answers to be exactly ordinary. Besides, what did she expect if she assigned words that weren't ordinary?

Discreet. A friend who is discreet does not repeat your secrets. The fingers wrote swiftly on.

Tee smiled happily as she stretched out on her bed to watch. In what seemed no time at all, the shabti came to the end of the page of math problems and stood to face her, and bow. Then, as abruptly as it had appeared, it was gone: no puff of smoke, no transporter-shimmer, no flash-bang, just gone.

Tee lay back on her bed and stared at the ceiling. After a moment she picked up *Jessica Jackson and the Map of Mandilore*. Only when she opened it and had to peer at the pages did she realize that the room had grown too dark for reading. "You'll ruin your eyes," Grandma Smitz would have said. She sat up to turn on the bedside light, then crossed to the table to turn on the desk lamp, too. Looking out, she saw that the cloudy sky had darkened like a storm sky back home in New England, and was threatening rain. In the desert? At this time of year? Pulling the casement half shut, Tee lay down again and began to read where she had left off the night before. The story was exciting, but she kept losing the thread of a paragraph and having to start over again at the beginning. Something was niggling at the back of her mind.

Hands. That was it. Something about the shabti's hands. Tee lowered the book and frowned. The shabti's fingers hadn't been stiff and stubby. They were pudgy, but not much pudgier than her own, and they had bent at the knuckles. She shivered. Why hadn't she noticed that right away? The shabti's arms were almost smooth. Its hair no longer looked carved-out-of-wood-and-painted, but like—like a wig made of masses of tiny, glossy braids. And the face—

The shabti had become a fuzzy copy of Leticia Ann Woodie. It was a cartoon of Tee herself, in Egyptian costume.

NINE

By the time the shabti reappeared after washing the supper dishes on Sunday evening, it looked even more real. In the moment before it vanished, Tee saw that its wig looked less wiggish and more like hair. In place of the pleated skirt and the blouse with bright embroidered neckline and short sleeves, it wore a blurry pair of jeans and a San Diego Zoo T-shirt. They weren't Tee's. They were ones it had magicked up. Tee's mind raced as she rolled the small wooden figure up in its bit of bubbly plastic wrap and tucked it back into its box. It was going to end up *exactly* like her, just like Princess Maatkare's shabti in a picture in one of Great-uncle Bass's books. Except for the mummy wrappings from the waist down, that shabti could have been its princess's twin sister.

The problem was that Tee could talk to hers, but when it answered, Tee couldn't understand more than a word here and there. She needed to be able to talk *with* it. If she didn't know what it didn't understand, how could she tell what to teach it? She sat at the bedroom worktable, her chin propped on her hands, and stared hard at the box.

What it didn't know . . .

Tee suddenly blinked and sat up straight. How could the shabti *not* sound as if it had a mouth full of stones when it tried to speak English? Mr. Duran had said in class that the ancient Egyptians had hieroglyphs for most of the letter sounds in the alphabet, but not all of them. There were sounds they just didn't use. That meant the shabti didn't know how to *make* the sound for any letter that didn't have a hieroglyph to match it.

Tee pushed her chair back and hurried out into the hallway. The library door was open, and Charles was planted in front of the computer, watching a row of hieroglyphs click across the computer screen. Tee bit her lip. She wanted the Egyptian dictionary back, but Curious Charles was a problem. If he asked what she wanted it for, she couldn't explain, and not explaining would set Charles's nose to twitching.

He did not hear her come in.

Tee stepped over to the bookcase as quietly as she could. Squatting down on her heels, she pulled the dictionary from the bottom shelf, then ran a finger along the other books there until she came to a tall, slim volume with the title *The Afterlife of the Ancient Egyptians*. She blew the dust off the top in a quiet puff, and opened it. It had page after page of photographs of paintings of long lines of stiff gods and goddesses, and boats, and men and women striding beside a river. The river had ruler-straight banks with bends in it that were more like corners. Tee closed the book quickly. If the shabti ever saw it, everything would be spoiled. The longer it thought it had awakened in the Afterlife, and not three thousand or so years into the future, the better. Pulling out the next two books, she slipped *The Afterlife* in flat against the back of the shelf and replaced the others. Then she filled the gap with another from the end of the row. She held the *Dictionary of Ancient Egyptian* behind her back and went to peer over Charles's shoulder.

"What are you doing?"

Charles jumped, and the cursor skidded across the screen as his hand jerked across the mouse pad. "Don't *do* that. I almost lost the page."

"Why is that in hieroglyphics?" Tee asked uneasily. "Didn't your class start on the Romans today, too?

Charles kept his eyes on the screen. "Yeah, but that question I posted on the Egyptian archaeology bulletin board last week? Somebody's putting up another answer right now. They're in the middle of it."

"Oh." Tee was almost as wary of computers as she

was of the Spider Lady. "I guess I'll go, then." She backed out into the hall.

In her own room, Tee opened the *Dictionary* to the "Guide to Pronunciation" at the front. She ran a finger down the hieroglyphic alphabet from the eagle that was **A** to the quail chick that stood for **U,** to pick out the figures that matched ordinary alphabet sounds. There were hieroglyphs for all but five letters. She made a list of those five—the sounds the shabti could not read. She wrote them down in a column, capitals and small letters, printing and longhand side by side: C—c *C—c,* J—j *J—j,* and so on. Then she made a list of letters that had more than one sound.

When the lists were complete, she placed the shabti box in the center of the floor, lifted the top off, and stepped back quickly. "Shabti?"

As suddenly as ever, it stood before her, smoothly blank faced. It bowed, arms raising and lowering in respect, then stood as straight and stiff as before.

"Her Iee aam, m' Preen'ss," it said solemnly.

Tee swallowed nervously. Each time it appeared, she was almost as startled as the first time. "Shabti, you must learn to speak all the sounds of—of this-world-here's language so I can understand you." She took a deep breath. Talking to it was eerily like talking to yourself in a mirror and having the mirror-self never move or blink.

"Ss, Preen'ss As eohoo 'omman."

Tee pulled at her fingers nervously. "See, that's what I mean! I think you *think* you're talking English. I guess you are, but I can't tell what you're saying." She pointed to her list. "These are the letters you don't know the sounds for. Right? This one"—Tee jabbed a finger at the first letter—"this is C, like *see*. Sometimes its sound is hard like K, like in *cup*. When it's with H, the sound is *ch*, sort of like your Egyptian *Tch*.

"See. Kuh. Ch."

"Yes! And this one." She pointed at the D. "Its name is *dee*, and the sound is *duh*. *Duh*."

It was simple. The shabti didn't need to hear anything twice. It repeated the sound for each letter as Tee went down the list. It reeled them all off in one breath from C to Z with no mistake. Then it made another deep bow.

Tee hesitated. "Um, shabti? Maybe you'd better stop the bowing. People don't bow like that here—in this world, I mean. Maybe if you just nodded?"

The shabti nodded. "Have ee gain-ed the mahstery of leet-ters which ee-oh-oo rekooire, me Prinkess?"

It took only a moment for Tee to figure that one out. "Oh! Sort of," she answered. "But it's 're-*quire*.' And '*let*-ters' and 'Prin-*cess*.' And '*you*,' not 'e-oh-oo'."

"Yes, me Princess." The shabti crossed its hands on its breast and made a nod so deep that it was almost a bow. "Iyt ees good to beh ablee ayt layst toh speak, for there ees mooch ee do not oonderstand. May ee aysk ohf these thin-gus?"

Tee frowned as her ears and brain strained to turn the mangled words into familiar ones. "I guess so," she said warily. "What things?"

The shabti spoke woodenly. "Ee woold ask whee does meh princess slip een so small and pleen a chamber?" If Tee had not been trying so hard to understand, she might have thought the blank eyes almost watchful. "Eef theh peopleh een thees hoose ayre her keet-chen and hoosehold servaynts, whee es sheh asked toh do theh-eer work? And whee ees the clothin-guh een thee Netherworld so oogly? Wheer are the guh-arments of fine coht-ton and leenen, and ohr-nay-ments ohf guh-old and lapis and cor-nehlian promeesed toh theh royale dead? These thin-gus were wreeten een theh sarcop-hagoos een wheech weh wehr laid een theh tomb. All these thin-gus ee do not oonderstand."

Tee's eyes squinted, and her nose wrinkled up in concentration. She thought she got the gist of what the shabti was saying. The shabti thought her family were her servants. It could not understand why she was expected to do things like wash the dinner dishes. Princess Tee-something should be living in a palace and wearing beautiful clothes and gold and jewels like the ones that were buried with her. Tee tried desperately to think of an answer that would make sense, but couldn't. Instead, she took a deep breath and said, "I don't understand, either."

It was certainly the truth, even if not exactly in the way the shabti meant. Even with her peek into Great-uncle Bass's old book, what Tee knew of what the ancient Egyptians believed about life in the Netherworld after they were dead would have fit into a thimble with room left over. She was afraid to try to make up an explanation. Every straight-out lie she had ever told had snuck back to bite her in the ankle when she wasn't looking. She slipped off the bed. "Maybe you'd better go away for now," she told the stocky figure in its ancient finery. "I need to think."

The shabti nodded. In a blink it was only a small wooden doll propped against a painted Egyptian box on the carpet.

Outside, the heavy air stirred. It really was going to rain. A breeze ruffled the curtains, and sent a spray of drizzle across the windowsill. Tee hurried to move the box to the top of the bookcase and went back to reach across the table and pull the casement shut.

Hurrying footsteps sounded on the stairs, and Mrs. Woodie's voice called from the hall, "Tee? Check the windows in the library and Charles's room, will you?"

Mr. Woodie was out in the garage, moving boxes to make room to bring the car in out of the storm. If it was left out, a leak at the top of the windshield made a hanging puddle collect and bulge downward in the cloth roof-lining, right over the driver's head. He came in the front door, dripping water from his old rain hat and coat, as Tee reached the foot of the stairs.

"What say, Princess? Good night for a fire in the fireplace?" He hung his hat and coat up on the old-fashioned coatrack beside the door.

"And ghost stories!" Charles called from the living room, where he had his tiny tin Civil War soldiers and little bottles of enamel paints spread out on newspapers on the floor. Across the room, the Sunday-evening rerun of *Star Trek: Voyager* was interrupted by a weather announcement moving across the bottom of the screen:

" . . . heavy rains throughout the night, with the possibility of thunderstorms, clearing Monday morning. Flash flood warnings will be in effect until mid-afternoon . . ."

"Ghost stories, yes, fire no. Ugh! I *hate* thunderstorms." Mrs. Woodie appeared in the doorway and crossed to the fireplace to make sure the chimney damper was closed. She always laughed about Grandma Smitz being afraid that lightning would travel down the chimney or through the TV cable and zap everyone in the room, but at the first rumble of thunder she always changed her tune to "better safe than sorry." Once a storm drew close, she unplugged the TV and sat with her feet tucked up under her in her armchair, off the floor. "Anyone for hot chocolate with the ghost stories?" she asked.

Charles's hand and his father's shot up in the middle of the question.

"Great. You, too, Tee? I'll make a big thermos full now so we don't need to have the stove on later."

"Mmm, I guess so," Tee answered absently from the sofa. She was watching the "away team" on a shuttle struggle to escape an ion storm, but not seeing them. She was thinking about what a wet Monday might mean: gym class indoors instead of on the playground or ball field. Team relays for somersaults. For chin-ups. Walking the balance bar. Cartwheels. Somersaults scared her, but at least she could do them. Or do one, anyway. Connie Tayler could chin herself on the crossbar, but Tee could never even pull her feet off the floor. Or walk even the low balance bar without falling off. Cartwheels were terrifying. Humiliating. In her cartwheels, her feet lifted only about a foot off the ground. If only she could send the shabti in her place! It probably could spin cartwheels for hours on end if she told it to, but what good was that if it looked as blank as a zombie and didn't dare open its mouth?

She sighed. The starship *Voyager* crew had it easy with their Universal Translator. It made even the weirdest aliens automatically speak English. You weren't supposed to notice that they spoke English when they were on their own ships or planets even when *Voyager* and its crew were light-years away. The writers, she thought, ought to make them speak their own language, with the English in subtitles across the bottom of the screen. That's what the shabti needed. Subtitles. In a suddenly silly mood, she imagined a Teletubby screen planted in the shabti's middle on which to run them.

A sudden crash of thunder and loud drumming of rain against the living room window brought Mrs. Woodie running to switch off the television and pull its plug. Mr. Woodie turned out the lights.

The hot chocolate and ghost stories were delicious. Afterward, though, Tee could not have repeated a single story. Her head was so full of tomorrow that each story went in one ear, gave her a small, pleasant shiver, and flew right out the other. Back up in her room at bedtime, she switched off her light and slipped under the covers with her heart thumping with dread.

It was no ordinary Monday-morning-is-almost-here-and-I-feel-sick sort of dread. It was fingertip-tingling, and almost delicious.

She had decided she *was* going to take the shabti to gym class.

TEN

Mr. Woodie looked up from his newspaper. "Tee, stop stirring your cereal and *eat* it."

Tee, feeling fizzy with fright and excitement, looked at the bowlful of cereal she had stirred into a pinkish, soupy glop, and felt her stomach tighten in disgust. She reached for her glass of orange juice, but her throat tightened at the first sip, and she almost burped it up again. "My stomach feels funny," she announced. "Can't I just eat a piece of toast instead?"

Her mother popped another slice of bread in the toaster then reached over to feel Tee's forehead. "Well, you're not feverish. Does your head feel stuffy? I don't want you going out in wet weather if you're coming down with something. I can stay home for the day."

"No!" Tee sat up in alarm. "I feel fine. I *have* to go to school."

Her father looked at her over the rim of his paper. "You *have* to go?" To her mother he said dryly, "Are you sure she doesn't have a fever, Sally?"

Charles looked up from checking the computer printout of his history homework and made a face of silly surprise. "Mama, Mama, the sky is falling!" he squeaked.

"Oh, dry up," Tee said with a sniff. "I'm ignoring you." She took a bite of the piece of toast their mother passed to her, then decided she might be able to take a little scrape of butter after all. And . . .

"Here." Charles pushed the pot of strawberry jam across the table as a peace offering. "Teesha, can I maybe borrow your Egyptian doll again, to take to class? When I gave my report on the hieroglyphics, Mrs. Wersba asked what a shabti looks like. Can I? Borrow it, I mean?"

Tee almost dropped her toast. Quickly, she took another big bite of it to hide her alarm. When she answered, it was with a nervous shrug and what she hoped sounded like boredom. "Maybe. Maybe I'll show it to my social studies class first."

"Sure," Charles said, sneaking a look at Tee over the rim of his juice glass. She didn't seem to realize that she was doing little bounces up and down on her chair. Their mother noticed, too.

"Tee, if you have to go to the bathroom, hurry up and go. Daddy and I are going to drive you to school this morning so you won't have to wait out in the rain for the bus. No? Well, if you're finished eating, clear your dishes and put on your rain boots and poncho. You, too, Charles."

"Five minutes, everyone," Mr. Woodie called as he left the kitchen.

Tee kept her backpack on under her rain poncho in the car, sitting uncomfortably forward with the safety belt too tight across her middle. At school she kept it on all the way to Mrs. Chatto's room.

Instead of lockers, the school had an old-fashioned cloakroom for each classroom. They had long rows of coat hooks for coats. Below, above the lined-up rain boots was a row of hooks for backpacks. As soon as she found herself alone, Tee slipped a small parcel from her backpack into one deep skirt pocket. Her *Jessica Jackson* paperback went into the other. She had chosen the navy blue skirt with the deepest pockets so they would not make too big a bulge. She slipped her hand in to touch the plastic-wrapped parcel, then took up her books.

In English class, the first fifteen minutes—"read-aloud time" on Mondays—turned into pure misery at the very start.

"This week before we go to the library," Mrs. Chatto told the class, "we're going to sample *My Friend*

Mr. Leakey, which was written by a famous scientist named J. B. S. Haldane."

Someone in the back of the room groaned. Mrs. Chatto ignored the groan. "Let's see—Tee? You haven't had a turn as reader yet. Come on up."

Numbly, Tee made her way to the front of the room and took the open book from Mrs. Chatto. It was an old book, and had been read so often that the corners of the pages were rounded and the paper felt soft. Tee was so nervous that at first she couldn't see the words clearly. When they cleared and her eyes skipped down the first page, she felt sure that she must be scrambling the words up in her brain. Why would a famous scientist be writing about a magician turning a cow into a grandfather clock? She swallowed hard, and began to read. "I have had some—"

"Speak up, Tee. I don't think Eddie and Rodney can hear you in the back." Mrs. Chatto raised her own voice. "Is that what you were saying to Rodney, Eddie?"

Eddie Duran, confused, looked around for some sign or hint of what the question meant. When no helpful whisper came, he put on a hopeful smile and said, "Yes, miss. I guess."

"All right, Tee. This time read it loudly enough to reach the back tables."

Tee tried, but her throat was so tight that she was sure she must sound like a crow with laryngitis. It was a silly book—goofy-silly—and when she came to the part about the embroidered curtains in Mr. Leakey's room with pictures on them that changed if you looked away and then looked back, she was back to a near whisper.

Mrs. Chatto sighed. "Thank you, Tee. Let's give someone else a chance. Eddie read last week, so—Rodney, will you come up and read a few paragraphs?"

While Rodney read, Tee sat with her eyes on her desktop and her left hand touching the bump in her pocket that was the shabti. *If only it could do the standing up in front of everyone and the reading aloud. The silly thing can read English now. Why does it have to sound like a talking stick?*

The next thing she knew, the class was lining up to go to the library, and Mrs. Chatto was saying, "All right, let's go now, and quiet in the halls, please."

Tee loved the library visits even though the shelves were half empty and some of the books almost as old as Grandma Smitz. Miss Marter, the aide, announced a contest for the best poster for National Book Week in November, and pinned the contest rules up on the bulletin board. After that, everyone was *quiet*, or just whispered, unless they were talking to Mrs. Chatto or Miss Marter. No one bothered anyone. No one asked anyone to stand up in front of the class and talk about the book he or she checked out last week.

Tee stood in line to return *Anne of Avonlea* and *Lad with a Whistle*, and then went straight to the fiction shelves, where she had decided to work her way through from AIKEN TO ZINDEL. At two books a week, skipping only the ones that were about everyday life and the ones she had read before she came to Oasis Wells, she figured that she ought to be past PYLE or even STEVENSON by the end of the school year. Library period was perfect for skimming the first chapters of books, to save carrying home three quarters of a pound of boredom by mistake. She had reached the end of the C-authors, and when it was time to check out books, got in line with *The Night-Watchmen* and *Emma Tupper's Diary*.

Math class started out better than usual because the Spider Woman had sprained her ankle over the weekend. That meant that she stayed at her desk or propped up against the blackboard chalk tray all period instead of roaming around and pouncing. Tee always sat behind Devoe Hopper, the biggest boy in class, and as long as Mrs. Raymond was sitting down, Tee could stay out of sight behind Devoe by sliding down in her chair and keeping her head bent.

Mrs. Raymond tapped a steel-colored fingernail on the little Chinese brass gong on her desk. "Ears up, Jackrabbits! Instead of collecting your homework assignments, I'd like each of you, starting with Audra here, to pass your paper to the person on your right. James, you're the last at the back, so you'll bring yours up to Audra."

She waited, tapping the steel fingernails on her desktop while the papers rustled from hand to hand.

"Good. Now you can all play Teacher for a while and check the answers on the paper your next-door-neighbor just gave you. If you think one is wrong, mark it with a check. When you're finished, write your own name at the bottom of the paper and pass it along the row and up to me."

Tee took one long, desperate last look at the shabti's page of fraction problems as she handed it on to Alison Tanny, and squeezed her eyes tight shut as if that would make the answers stick in her brain. The funny thing was that it seemed to work. As she stared blankly at Gary Mandelson's paper, for half a second it was almost as if she were seeing both papers at the same time. Gary's number five was wrong. It was wrong, that is, if the shabti was right, and of course it *was*. Pleased, Tee marked a small, neat check beside the wrong answer, signed her name at the bottom, and passed in the paper.

Her pleasure soon turned to alarm. The Spider Woman riffled through the papers. Beginning with the first problem, she asked Katie Schumacher to come up to the blackboard to show how she knew that nine people sharing four pizzas would get more pizza than six people sharing two pizzas. When problem five came up, it was Tee's turn. "Where *is* Tee?"

Tee's hand inched up reluctantly as everyone looked in her direction.

"Hiding again, Tee? Don't worry. You were right to mark number five wrong on the paper you corrected. The problem was: 'If Jack and eleven of his friends are sharing four pizzas at one long table and Ellen and seventeen of her friends are sharing six pizzas at another table, which table would you rather be sitting at if you were really hungry?' Now, can you tell us how you found the answer, Tee?"

"I don't know," Tee whispered.

"What was that? I didn't hear."

"I don't know," Tee muttered unhappily. "By mummbr, I guess," she mumbled.

The Spider Woman put a hand to her ear. "Was that, 'By mumble, I guess,' or 'By guess, I guess?' Guesses do work sometimes, but they're just as likely to let you down. Audra, can you tell us how *you* found the right answer?"

Tee shrank down behind Devoe in resentful misery.

Tee scowled when she opened her lunch box and found a fat ham sandwich on rye bread, a bunch of grapes, and a mini carton of apricot nectar. She hated rye bread; the grapes were the kind with seeds; and apricot nectar was too sticky-sweet. She picked out and ate the ham, and traded the nectar for Charles's apple juice. The bread, and most of the grapes, she scraped into the cafeteria waste bin.

Art class—Tee's favorite, after English on library-visit day—was fine until just before the bell. Mrs. Rodriguez, the county art teacher who came to Oasis Wells one day a week, had put out sketch paper, poster paper, water jars, and watercolor paints on the tables along the window wall of the cafeteria, where the class met. They were to work on ideas for the Book Week poster contest and then draw and paint them on posters to put up in the main hall after the Halloween decorations came down.

Tee forgot all about the shabti in her pocket. She drew a dragon sleeping in his cave on top of a great heap of coins and cups and gems and jewels, and a tiny figure tiptoeing away with a big, two-handled cup. Above the cave shadows, she made an arch of capital letters spelling out BOOK WEEK, and beneath the drawing, NOVEMBER 12-17. Miss Mackintosh came to peer over her shoulder. "That's great! Is it Bilbo Baggins and Smaug from *The Hobbit*?"

Tee nodded shyly.

Mrs. Rodriguez looked at her watch. "You'd better start copying it onto your poster paper now, Tee, or there won't be time to paint the shadows in the cave or color in the gold and jewels. You're going to make it bigger, aren't you? It's very tiny."

Tee nodded again, but somehow as Bilbo and the dragon and gold and shadows and lettering took shape on the poster paper—even though they were a bit larger—they ended up huddled in the center of a large white space.

When the class bell rang, the posters were spread out on an empty table to dry. Rodney Ankrum pointed to Tee's and gave a snort. "That's not a poster. It's a postcard. If it was on a wall, you'd have to get a telescope to read it."

Tee loved the picture and thought it was better than any of the others. She almost hit Rodney. Afterward, she had to fight all the way to her locker to keep from crying, and from her locker to gym class.

In the large multipurpose room that became a gymnasium when it wasn't being the auditorium or an extra classroom, the gymnastics equipment was already set up. Exercise mats covered the middle part of the floor. Three classes of girls sat on the folding chairs along the walls changing into gym shoes, or stood in little groups wrestling shorts on under their skirts. They pulled the skirts off over their heads or dropped and stepped out of them.

"Hurry it up, girls!" Mrs. Amery called. "You're wasting time. The doors are shut. There aren't any boys around to spy, so you don't need to be so shy. Neela Taggart, Cindy Trussell, some of you others—get those chairs back against the wall."

Tee had chosen a chair half hidden beside the piano, in the far corner. Clutching her shoes and shorts to her chest, she waited nervously for everyone to be looking in another direction and when the chance came, slipped into the triangle of space behind the old upright piano. There she knelt to unroll her shorts and undo the shabti parcel inside. *"Shabti?"* she whispered.

"Ee ahm here f'r you, me Princess." The shabti looked around for Tee at eye level, then looked down as Tee tugged at its skirt. It gave a deep nod and straightened to stand, as it always did, straight as a stick.

"Tee Woodie! What on earth are you doing back there?" Mrs. Amery's voice rang out loudly. The room fell still.

"Dressing, Mrs. Amery." Tee's timid voice trembled as she looked up at the shabti standing over her. Flustered, she tried by pointing to the shoes and shorts to make it understand what it had to wear. "Hurry!" she hissed. "Put on the shorts and shoes and go take my place in the—in the games. Someone will pick me—you, that is—for a team. Do everything in the same order everyone else does. They have to think you're me."

Mrs. Amery scowled and planted her fists on her hips, but then sighed and tried to speak softly. "Dressing. Well, we're waiting. *Now*, Tee! You're on team four, over here. We'll do relays first."

"Ee come," the shabti said.

"Shorts! Shorts and shoes," Tee hissed. "And don't say anything. Not one word!"

The shabti stepped out from behind the piano and walked calmly to join the end of team four's line.

Behind the piano, Tee, her eyes squeezed tight shut, sat clutching the shorts and tennis shoes to her chest. It was happening too fast, and now it was too late to stop it. But why hadn't Mrs. Amery exploded at the sight of the shabti-Tee's strange costume? Fearfully, Tee crept over to peer out into the room.

The shabti—magically dressed in blouse, shorts, and tennis shoes—stood in line looking exactly like Tee Woodie, or at least like Tee Woodie imitating a fence post. The girls on each team jumped up and down, cheering each other on, but it only watched, blank-faced. Each time a girl at the head of the line stepped forward onto the mat, the shabti moved up one place as if it had been going to gym class twice a week forever. Tee watched, wide-eyed, and held her breath.

"Next!" Mrs. Amery called. "Same thing. Three somersaults going, a cartwheel coming back, then go to the rear of the line."

Team five fell silent. Connie Tayler nudged another girl.

Tee watched with her hands clapped over her mouth. She saw the Other Tee step forward, kneel, put hands and head down, and push itself heels-over-head in three awkward somersaults. They were awkward, but at least went in a straight line and didn't end up off the mat. Standing, the Other Tee turned on its heel, put its arms up, teetered a little, then turned an almost-straight-armed, almost-straight-legged cartwheel.

It was a moment before team four realized they had pulled ahead of the others, and burst into cheers. Tee, her heart thumping like a kettledrum, drew back into her cubbyhole behind the piano. She wanted to watch, and didn't want to watch. A magical shabti ought to be able to do whatever it was told to, but hers was uncomfortably doofus-ish. Being magical, it ought to be perfect, spinning through the air with the greatest of grace and leaving everyone openmouthed with surprise. Maybe the ancient Egyptians didn't do somersaults or turn cartwheels.

Tee sighed, and tried to ignore the sounds of running and jumping feet on the mats, and the cheers. Taking *Jessica Jackson and the City Beneath the City* from her skirt pocket, she tried to read while, out on the floor, the Other Tee hopped from one end of the room to the other on its right foot and back on the left, and teetered along the low balance beam without falling off. Almost falling, but not quite.

If anyone had been looking, they might have imagined that the corners of its mouth began to twitch stiffly upward.

ELEVEN

After school, Tee hung back in the shade of the cottonwood trees in front of the school while Charles clowned around with Tony Okimbo at the bus stop on the corner. Charles would need only one look to know something was up. Pretending that nothing had happened would only make it worse. Charles was as curious as a boxful of beagle puppies, and when he smelled a secret, he could be more pestiferous than the Godzilla of all mosquitos. The thought of Charles as a giant mosquito hovering up against the ceiling outside of her bedroom door made Tee giggle out loud.

The nearest of the students waiting for the bus turned to stare. Connie Tayler and Marilu Purdom whispered together. Tee, flushed red and frozen-faced, stared off up the road as if the giggle hadn't been hers at all.

* * *

At home, sitting on the edge of her bed with the shabti back in its box and the box back on the table, Tee sat with her chin on one hand. Magic was much more work than it was supposed to be. If she couldn't find some magic of her own to get rid of the shabti's weird accent, she wouldn't dare send it anywhere, not even to gym class again. She scowled across the room at the top shelf of her bookcase, where the Jessica Jackson story she had been reading in gym class sat atop the others waiting to be returned to the public library. She planned to return all six tomorrow and get another six. Her scowl deepened—and then she blinked.

Her answer was on the next shelf down, where *Winnie the Pooh* lived between a tattered paperback *Velveteen Rabbit* and *The Twelve Dancing Princesses*. When she was five and quarantined with the measles, her father had grown weary of reading *Pooh* aloud over and over again, and brought home a tape of it for her to fall asleep to after he had read his share. She still had the tape somewhere, and the tapes of *The Chronicles of Narnia* that Great-uncle Bass had sent one Christmas. If the shabti could follow the words on the page and hear how they were pronounced at the same time, problem solved! She could read a book aloud to it herself, but that would be a dead bore. On second thought, she decided that the Narnia tapes wouldn't work. The actor reading them had an English accent.

None of her tapes were in the bookcase. After a flurry of searching through the boxes in the closet, she found them in one of the shoe boxes up on the high shelf. The *Pooh* and the *Narnia* tapes she left in the box. The two others were *Little Women* and *A Wizard of Earthsea*. She chose *Little Women*. It was old-fashioned, but it had more useful names and words. Finding the tape recorder was more difficult. Tee went to ask Charles, but he hadn't seen it since the family left Maine. It wasn't in the library, or in any of the unpacked mover's cartons in two of the spare bedrooms.

When Mrs. Woodie arrived home at five o'clock, she found Tee rummaging in the dining room sideboard. "Now, why would we keep the tape recorder in with the good dinner dishes?"

"I don't know," Tee said glumly. "I looked everyplace else."

"I think your dad put the slide and movie projectors in the cupboard under the TV and VCR. He might have stuck the tape recorder in there, too. Have you looked?"

"Found it!" Tee called a moment later from the living room. In a flash, she was out and taking the stair steps two at a time.

With a chair propped up under her doorknob, as usual, Tee awakened the shabti. "Here I am," it said, and it put its hands together, with its usual polite nod.

Tee watched it curiously, but it didn't even blink at hearing the shiny black, flat box speak up and say, "*'Christmas wouldn't be Christmas without any presents,' grumbled Jo,*" when Tee pressed the Play button. Its expression was as blank as always until it understood that the words it heard were the words Tee's finger pointed out as it moved along the lines. At that, a tiny shiver of movement shimmered across its face and vanished. It reached out a stiff forefinger and began to follow the voice on the tape along the lines of print by itself.

Startled, Tee snatched back her own hand. Perhaps she had imagined that almost invisible shiver of surprise. Its eyebrows hadn't raised a hair. The corners of its mouth hadn't twitched. Vaguely troubled, Tee watched for a while, but then stretched out on her bed and settled down to enjoy *Little Women*. She had seen the movie with Winona Ryder as Jo twice on video, but it had been a long time since she had read it. She had forgotten how interesting it was.

The tape stopped.

"My Princess?"

Tee sat up in alarm. The shabti had its finger on the Stop button.

"My Princess, explain please to your servant what is '*statirical*'?"

"'Statirical?'" Tee got up to look. "Oh, that's Amy's mistake for 'satirical,' like in 'making fun of.'"

The shabti nodded woodenly. "I thank you, my Princess." It pushed the Play button. Julia Norman's voice began again in mid-sentence with "' . . . *and improve your vocabilary,' returned Amy with dignity.*"

Tee giggled and sank back on her pillow, but it was a while before she could settle down to listening again. A moment later there was another sudden silence, another "My Princess," and another question.

After the fourth "My Princess," Tee grew impatient and, after the seventh, irritable. "You don't need to know what snow is," she said grumpily. "Just the sound of the words." It was only after ten minutes of listening without interruption to the reader, Julie Norman, that it dawned on Tee: Each of the shabti's irritating questions had sounded more and more normal—more like Julia Norman.

"Shabti, stop!"

The shabti pressed the Stop button. "I hear, my Princess."

Tee sat up and thought for a moment. "Shabti, if you're going to do *all* my work, you have to sound like me, not her." She crossed to the table. "I'll read some to you. Show me where you stopped."

The shabti pointed to the middle of a sentence two thirds of the way down the page. Tee saw that its fingers now had perfect fingernails, and little creases at the knuckles. That was good, she told herself, but it didn't stop it from being creepy. She began reading at " . . . *while the December snow fell quietly without, and the fire crackled cheerfully within* . . ." She got as far as "chrysanthemums and Christmas roses bloomed in the windows" and had to stop. The shabti was leaning close to watch Tee's finger move from word to word as she read. Every time their arms brushed, the hair on Tee's arms and the back of her neck stood straight up. In the end it was just too weird.

Tee closed the book with a snap. She put it down and edged away toward the bed. "*Little Women* isn't such a good idea," she said quickly. "It's too old-fashioned. We can just talk. You can copy what I sound like. Go sit down."

The shabti hesitated. "It is not fitting for a servant to sit in the presence of my Princess," it said stiffly.

"Oh—just *sit*," Tee snapped as she plumped down on the edge of her bed.

It sat on the chair by the table, its back broomstick-straight, its hands crossed neatly in its lap.

Tee felt more uncomfortable than before. There was an awkward silence. Then, suddenly, a question that had popped into her head days earlier popped unexpectedly out of her mouth. "Shabti, what goes on in your head when you're in your box?" She pointed at the painted box. "I mean—do you think about things?"

The shabti's face was as wooden as the first time Tee saw it. "I do not know what this question means. Here I am. When I am not here, I am—not."

Tee tried another question. "What do you remember from before you and—before we were, uh, buried? What princesses did, how they lived, and all that?"

A shadow of a frown flickered faintly between the shabti's brows, but vanished too quickly for Tee to notice it. "I do not understand," it replied. "It was not"—it hesitated—"your servant was a nothing before it was awakened. It was a stick of wood."

Every try Tee made at conversation came to a similar dead end, so she gave up and began to talk about anything that came into her head. How she hated living in the desert. How she longed for really *green* trees, and for grass. How awful the house was, with all its dark corners and empty bedrooms, and the mouse smell that a dozen scrubbings still hadn't washed away. How no one at school liked her. What the teachers were like. How her old school was better, if not much. When at last she ran out of steam, she sat up straight and said, "Okay, now you read from the book. Out loud."

The shabti sat bolt upright at the table, holding the book in both hands, and began where the tape had left off. Except for an occasional correction—"It's *'Didn't,'* not 'did nit,'" for one—its pronunciation was almost perfect. It even managed to give the different characters different voices, instead of droning along on a single note. Tee changed from her school uniform into capris and a T-shirt while she listened. She was in the closet, changing her school shoes for her favorites, an almost-worn-to-bits pair of tennis shoes, when a knock came at the door.

"Tee?"

Tee froze. It was her mother's voice. She was home earlier than usual for a Tuesday. Before Tee could think what to do, she heard the doorknob turn, and the chair propped under it toppled over with a thump. She put the tennis shoes down gingerly and held her breath.

"What on earth are you doing in here? Talking to yourself?"

Tee was afraid to move for fear of bumping against the skates that hung inches away, on the one wall, or knocking over the stack of shoe boxes that leaned against the other. All she could do was crane her head around as far as it would go. Through the half-open closet door, she saw the shabti—now, suddenly, dressed in capris and a T-shirt—rise from the table, turn calmly, and nod. "I am practicing reading aloud," it said.

"Ah, *that's* what you wanted the tape recorder for. For English class? Good idea, but you'd better finish up for now. Daddy's going to be at least half an hour late for his turn at kitchen duty. Come down in five minutes or so, will you? You can set the table and then give me a hand with peeling apples for the pie I should have in the oven in ten minutes."

"I will." The shabti nodded.

Tee took a deep breath as she heard the door close, and scrambled to her feet and out of the closet. The shabti turned to face her. "Have I now learned to speak the language of the Netherworld as you require, my Princess? Shall I now do the schoolwork?"

"Not yet." Tee looked at it thoughtfully. It might talk a little like an old-fashioned book, but it *sounded* exactly like what she supposed she must sound like herself. An unexpected giggle rose in her throat. If only it could go to horrible-awful math class for her!

In the silence, the shabti gave a deep nod that was only an inch or two short of being a bow. "There is a thing your servant does not understand. Is it permitted to seek an answer of my Princess?"

"Yes, I guess," Tee said warily.

"Then, why did my Princess conceal herself behind a great box when her servant ran and tumbled in her place in the chamber of games? Are the others not the ordinary girls they appear to be? Is the mistress of games an evil woman? Are the girls the daughters of the enemies of the pharaoh, your father?"

"No, no," Tee said hastily. "It's—it's just better if they don't know you're my—um, substitute. None of them have magical servants."

The shabti gave a sharp, little cock of its head, like a curious bird. "Of what importance is that? A princess need not think of such matters."

"A shabti doesn't, either," Tee answered quickly. "You can go. My homework can wait until after supper."

"Then I shall go down the stairs now and do as the woman your servant said." The shabti's blank Tee-face flickered with what might have been the shadow of a frown. Tee was too spooked by the close call to notice. "No!" she said in alarm. "No, I'll do that." She could just imagine an apple-peeling shabti turning to her mother to ask what a pie was, or where all the other tomb servants were. "You go back to—wherever it is you go."

"Okay, my Princess," it said. "I'm going."

The shabti vanished in a blink, and Tee quickly stuffed the little wooden figure into its painted box and fitted its lid back on. Forgetting the chores waiting for her downstairs, she stretched out on top of the bedspread to think.

The shabti learned so fast! But exactly what was she teaching it *for*? Just in case somebody accidentally saw it washing the dinner dishes? The answer, growing louder and louder in her ear, had been in the back of her mind all along. *What if—what if she* could *send it to Mrs. Raymond's math class in her place?*

Only once. Truly, only once.

Tee pulled one of her throw pillows over her face to smother her giggles and drummed her heels on the bed.

TWELVE

She wouldn't do it, of course. She wasn't brave enough. Besides, she wouldn't be able to watch, so where was the fun in that? Or what if something went wrong, some horrible goof? She imagined the shabti nodding politely and saying, "Thank you for your praise, O Spider Lady"? The class would explode. Everyone and his fifteenth cousin would hear about it. Tee grew hot with embarrassment just thinking about all the whispers and giggles—and the principal's report to her parents that would follow.

Impossible or not, the math class daydream kept coming back. There was the Other Tee standing at the blackboard, looking Mrs. Raymond in the eye and answering every question calmly. . . . It was so delicious that on Tuesday morning Tee daydreamed it again in math class, which was a major mistake. She was halfway through having the shabti astonish Mrs. Raymond with an explanation of how much pizza each of six people would get if each got a fair share of twenty small pizzas when she was startled awake by the sharp *rap-tap-tap!* of shiny fingernails on her desk.

"Hel*lo-oh!*" the Spider Woman said as she covered question three on Tee's homework paper with her long fingers. "Anyone home?"

Tee jumped. "I—I didn't hear the question," she whispered.

"I asked, 'If when Henry came over to your house for dinner you had seven tenths of a strawberry pie, and Henry ate one fourth of it, how much did he eat?' You have the right answer on your paper, Tee. Can you work it out in your head, without looking?"

"No," Tee whispered in misery. Even if she had done the homework herself, she couldn't have worked it out in her head. She had to write things down on paper. She had to *see* them.

"Cheer up, Tee! Weren't you listening at all? There are at least five ways of finding the answer, and for most of them we need a pencil and paper. Anyone who can do problems in her head—or his head—is very lucky."

As Mrs. Raymond moved on along the row of desks, Tee's eyes wandered toward the cloakroom door at the front of the room. She had never seen inside . . . maybe there was a big, empty cupboard? Or a dark corner?

After her mother walked in on the shabti, Tee had become much more careful at home. She did not open the Egyptian box until after supper, in homework time, and then she made sure the door was wedged shut. Every time she shoved a chair up under the doorknob, she felt uneasy, but quickly pushed the feeling away. After all, she wasn't being disobedient. Her parents hadn't told her not to use her magical servant, and as long as they didn't know she had one, they couldn't.

She even did some of her own homework.

The reading bits were good. She enjoyed the stories in the English book, and the descriptions of life in ancient Rome, with its plays and chariot races and central heating and tales of gods and heroes. Besides, she read so fast that it was getting harder all the time to bring home enough library books to last through the week. When the school library aide told Mrs. Chatto that at least twice a week before lunch period Tee Woodie returned two books and checked out two more, Mrs. Chatto put her foot down. "Two books a week, Tee. You need to spend time on your homework and on your friends."

"Yes, Mrs. Chatto," Tee had mumbled.

It took an extra after-school trip to the public library with a bulging backpack—carrying six books there and another six home with her schoolbooks—to keep her supplied with secret messages, hidden staircases, stolen jewels, magical charms, haunted houses, mistaken identities, and lost treasures. In the evenings her shabti wrote out the answers to English and history workbook questions, did all of the math homework, and vanished. But Tee had learned one lesson: She was more cautious about the homework. When the shabti was back in its box, she read through the workbook pages to try to see what the steps between the math problems and their answers were. Why have a magical shabti—even if it meant hours of time saved and A's on all your homework—if all you could do in class was whisper, "I don't know."

On Wednesday morning, Tee managed to slip into the cloakroom in Mrs. Raymond's room, but the shallow storage cupboards were lined with shelves, most of them full. There was nothing anywhere else to hide in, or behind, or under. The janitor's supply room on the other side of the classroom was kept locked. Tee paused with her back to the janitor's door when she passed, and put a hand behind her to jiggle the doorknob, but it was always locked until after noon. That was when Mr. Sergey, the custodian, started his day's work. Secretly, Tee was relieved. If she found a hiding place, she might plan the next step, and a next and next. Might even do it, and that would be fatal. It wouldn't work. The shabti still acted too much like a stick even if it didn't sound like one anymore. She could work on that, but . . .

On Thursday between fourth and fifth periods Mr. Sergey was at work in the supply room. Tee stuck her head in for a second, saw him there, and fled. That one glimpse was enough, though. She had spied a heating and air-conditioning vent at the base of the side wall a few feet inside the door, only the thickness of a wall away from the vent in Mrs. Raymond's room. If Mr. Sergey didn't keep the storeroom door locked while he was out cutting the grass or down in the furnace room, or anywhere else, she might be able to listen through it even if she couldn't see through it. Since it always *was* locked, she was safe imagining herself, as brave as Jessica Jackson, crouching by the vent to spy on the Great Math Class Masquerade.

On Friday morning, the janitor's door clicked open when she jiggled the knob.

If it happened once, it could happen again. That evening after Tee and her family came home from dinner at the Steak Shack, Tee shut herself in her bedroom and began to write out a plan. The first item on the list was *Make shabti more real*. Step two was, *Explain math class to it*. She was too eager to set to work to decide what step three would be.

The shabti sat at the table, straight-backed, feet together, one hand holding the sheet of paper flat, the other grasping the pencil.

"No." Tee shook her head. "Here, I'll show you." As the shabti stood, Tee sat down and hunched over the table, her forearm holding the paper, head tilted, her knuckles cramped up as she held the pencil. Her feet were tucked under the chair, her ankles crossed as she wrote.

"I can do that," the shabti said.

It did, but the result was still as stiff as a stick figure. "Lower," Tee said. "And more bendy." It tried to scrooch down in the chair to make itself small, but it still looked uncomfortable.

It practiced raising its hand to give an answer. Its arm shot up as straight as a flagpole every time.

Tee drew a map of Mrs. Raymond's classroom to show it where she sat. From one glance at the names Tee had written on the little chair squares in the drawing, it learned them all: that Devoe sat in front of her, Gary on her right, Missy on the left, and all the way back to Rodney and Jason in the far corner. But it did everything with as blank-eyed and straight-faced a countenance as ever

Tee frowned. "Can you *try* to smile? Like this," She gave a self-conscious grin.

The shabti widened its mouth into a straight, thin line of a smile that looked more like *I am clenching my teeth* than *I am friendly* or *I am cheerful*.

Tee drew a deep breath. It was never going to work. Mrs. Raymond and the class might think it was Tee Woodie, but that Tee Woodie was suddenly weird as a wombat. She knew she ought to be relieved. The timid part of her really was, but the part of Tee that loved tales of adventure with daring girl heroes was miserable. Jessica Jackson had never had an adventure any weirder than "Lateesha Woodie and the Egyptian Box," not even in *Jessica Jackson and the Captive of*—of Whatsis. The difference was, Lateesha Woodie was a cowardly chicken.

"Go, now," she told the shabti abruptly, and turned away sharply. Behind her, the shabti crossed its arms on its breast and nodded obediently.

And smiled.

THIRTEEN

It took all the weekend, one video, a movie at the Oasis Empire, all the rest of *Behind the Mirror* and half of *West of the Moon* before, after midnight on Sunday, Tee forgot to be miserable and fell asleep under the covers with the flashlight still on. She awoke on Monday morning with a headache from sleeping half smothered under a sheet and two blankets. The alarm clock buzzed away like an angry, helicopter-sized bee.

"Unh-un-nh!" Tee moaned and groped a hand out from under the covers. It touched the nightstand and flapped up and down until it met the clock and batted down the alarm button. Then it drew slowly back under the bedclothes like a snail into its shell.

Five minutes later the snooze buzzer went off, and Tee sat up with a groan. Her head throbbed. It was still early in October, but already the early mornings were darker. To make sure that the alarm hadn't gone off too soon, she squinted up her eyes and switched the bedside lamp on and quickly off again. Her eyes were dazzled, but she made out the long hand on the ten and the small one near the seven.

On her third try, Tee managed to sit up. "I think I'm sick," she announced to the clock. The thought made her feel almost cheerful. If she was sick, she wouldn't have to go to school. Her mother would stay home to bring her toast and weak tea and put cold compresses on her head. Once she felt better, there would be orange juice and scrambled eggs, and fruit and fresh-baked chocolate chip cookies later. Delicious. . . . Her mouth watered, and when her stomach didn't heave at the thought of all that food, she knew she probably wasn't sick at all.

"Arr-rrgh!" She groaned, held her head, and fell back onto her pillow. "Why can't the silly shabti go to school for me?" She lay there taking deep breaths until, bit by bit, her head stopped pounding.

When she opened her eyes to check the clock, it said three minutes to eight, and the room was bright with morning.

"Oh, no!" She sprang up and dashed for the closet, shedding pajamas on the way and snatching clean underwear from her middle drawer. Her mother or father always called if she wasn't down before seven-fifteen, but she hadn't heard a thing. Why hadn't one of them come up, or sent Charles to check? They always did when—at least once a week—she turned off the alarm and went back to sleep to dream that she was getting up, dressing, and going down to breakfast. Maybe they had to leave for the shop early. . . .

Breakfast! There was no time for it now. Tee hopped across to the chair on one foot as she pulled a sock onto the other. Downstairs, just below her window, she heard the front door slam. Charles? Going out to the bus stop by himself, without a peep, leaving her chin-deep in trouble? What had she done this time to make him mad at her?

The front door slammed again, and then a car door. Car door? Tee hopped around to the side of the table in front of the window, one shoe on, one off, to peer out. The Woodies' car was just backing into view out the drive from the garage at the rear of the house. As Tee watched, her mother appeared, hurried around the car, and climbed into the passenger's seat. Baffled, Tee reached for the window latch to undo it, raise the window, and call. Then she stopped, her hand frozen on the latch.

Up the lane, thirty or so yards from the corner of State Road, Charles—and someone—were running for the bus stop.

Tee stared after them, her forehead pressed against the glass. The school uniform, the dark hair hanging in a fat tail at one side . . .

Tee's hand went slowly to her own sleep-messy hair. She frowned, then suddenly whirled, knocking over an empty water glass. The shabti box was in its usual spot on the worktable, but her schoolbooks and backpack were gone. It had to be the shabti. What other explanation was there? Why else would her books be gone? She picked up the box gingerly and lifted the lid to peer in.

It was empty, of course. The shabti had put the lid back on before it left. That was odd, but Tee scarcely noticed. Slowly, dimly, the buzz of the snooze alarm came back to her. She had thought . . . no, she had *said* it. *"Why can't the silly shabti go to school for me?"*

Tee turned back to the window to watch helplessly as her father backed the car out into the lane. Through the cottonwoods she caught a glimpse of the North State Road bus at the stop by the three tall palm trees up at the corner. Then it pulled away from the bus stop and out of sight down the main road.

It was her own fault, but even if she had wakened in time to catch her parents or Charles before they left, what could she have done? Dash downstairs, shouting, "Stop! That's not me!"? She imagined her father shaking his head and saying automatically, "It's 'not *I*,' Tee," before being struck speechless at the sight of two Tees. She could just hear herself explaining, *"I haven't done my own homework for two weeks. My magical servant does it for me. It's true! See—I can make it go back in its box. GO!"*

She could go to school today for herself, of course. The front door was in full view of the secretary's desk in the office, but she could slip around and in the side door. She could hide in the girls' room nearest Mrs. Chatto's room. After the bell for the end of first period rang, she could catch the shabti in the hall. Before anyone saw two Tees for longer than a blink, it would be a wooden doll again, and safe in her pocket. She looked at the clock. The second morning bus was due in twenty-four minutes. It would be a different driver, so she could just say that she had missed the earlier bus. That was perfectly true—and she still had time to brush her teeth and eat breakfast.

Down in the kitchen, the breakfast dishes were still in the sink. The dishwasher Mrs. Woodie wanted to order was still waiting for Mr. Woodie to take out one of the old under-counter cupboards to make room for it. Perhaps next weekend, Tee thought as she filled a bowl with cereal. No more dishwashing! She almost dropped the milk carton when she remembered that she hadn't washed dishes herself in weeks. Her own dishwasher was a two-legged magical one. Next to it, a shiny new dishwasher was about as exciting as a—as an electric toothbrush. She poured herself a glass of orange juice, sat down with a *plump!* on the bench in the breakfast nook, and ate her cereal glumly. It was too sweet, the orange juice too sour. The whole milk was all gone, so the milk was skimmed. "Blue" milk. She hated it. Reluctantly, she looked up at the kitchen clock. Startled, she swallowed the rest of the orange juice down in one long breath and hurried out into the front hall, and stopped.

The bus was due in seven minutes. Bus pass. It wasn't in either skirt pocket, so it had to be in her backpack. Or *it* was using it! Tee raced upstairs, fished a handful of coins out of the little blue bowl on top of her bookcase, and hurried down again. As she ran, she was muttering out loud to the still-distant bus driver, "Don't-be-early-Don't-be-early-*Please*-don't-be-early!"

Her hand was on the front-door doorknob when she heard a car door slam in the driveway at the side of the house.

Through the sheer curtains at a dining room window, Tee saw her mother halfway to the front door. In a panic, she raced for the kitchen. Why was she here? Mrs. Woodie always checked the shop inventory and placed the orders for new tapes and CDs and DVDs first thing in the morning. Then she went to the bank with the money that had come in the evening before, after the late-afternoon bank deposit. The bank wasn't open yet, and it wasn't lunchtime, so why was she here?

Listening from inside the pantry off the kitchen, Tee suddenly felt as dim-witted as a goofy cartoon character with a lightbulb going on in a balloon over its head. First she heard the sounds of dishes being washed, and after a while the wheezy roar of the vacuum cleaner going back and forth in the dining room, and then the living room. Just because she never saw her mother cleaning house, had she thought that brownies did it?

She was trapped. She could hear her mother vacuuming her way up the stairs. Where was she supposed to hide? She couldn't slip up the back stairs, to go shut herself in her own closet. Her closet was carpeted, so her mother would probably vacuum there, too. That left the cellar.

The door to the cellar stairs was at the back of the pantry, opposite the door to the back stairs. Tee made her way carefully down the dusty, creaky steps. At the bottom, she paused to listen for a moment to be sure that the vacuum cleaner was still running somewhere above, then looked around her.

The cellar was one of the parts of the house the family hadn't cleared out yet, or cleaned. It lay under only the middle part of the house, so there were no windows, only air vents. It wasn't large, but it was fairly empty—surprising for Great-uncle Bass. Bare storage shelves, some with a few ancient-looking jars and cans on them, lined one wall. Three rows of empty wine racks stood along the rear wall. There were side-by-side cupboard doors set into the wall beyond the stairs. One cupboard was empty, and the other held some kind of machinery that resembled one of the weird contraptions Charles used to make with Build-A-Toy snap-together parts, except that this one was of iron, and disgusting looking—greasy on its undersides, and thick with dust on the top bits.

In the middle of the floor, an ancient wicker sofa huddled among boxes and crates of books, under a dusty, torn old bedspread. Tee peeled back the bedspread gingerly, covering her nose against the dust, and stretched out on the hard sofa cushion. From the nearest box she pulled a book called *The Submarine Chums at Sea*, dusted it off with a tail end of the bedspread, and settled down to read.

The Submarine Chums was almost interesting. Sort of. At least, the story made Tee forget to worry about the tangle of trouble the shabti-Tee might be getting her into at school. The way boys talked eighty or ninety years ago in adventure books was funny—stuffy and slangy at the same time, and stiff and polite around grown-ups. Stuffy or not, she was stuck with the submariners. All of the other books in the boxes were heavy, dull-looking volumes in tiny print.

The sound of the car starting up when her mother left again for the video shop didn't come until one o'clock: much too late to do anything about school. The bus ran only until mid-morning, and from mid-afternoon until just after six.

Two peanut-butter sandwiches, one glass of milk, half a bag of corn chips, the first half of a video, and an hour of fidgeting later, Tee heard the first sounds of voices and raced to her bedroom window. Charles's funny foghorn hoot of a laugh rang out before she caught sight of him. Then there he was, hop-skipping backward along the lane outside the waist-high stone wall that ran around the whole of Great-uncle Bass's house and grounds. *Their* house and grounds. He was waving his hands as he talked to her—to it. The shabti walked along with Tee's backpack clutched to its chest. *Probably couldn't unstiffen its arms enough to put it on the right way*, Tee thought grumpily. At least nothing too very awful could have happened at school. Charles looked as if he was being his ordinary irritating self, not someone whose sister had been sent to the principal's office for acting like a creature from another planet.

Watching it was creepy. It followed Charles in through the gate and along the Woodies' front walk, listening, and nodding: a perfect Tee except that the shabti looked calmly sure of itself.

Tee shivered.

Just before the shabti vanished beneath the porch roof under Tee's window, she saw it say something and grin a mechanical flicker of a grin quick as a camera flash.

It *did* learn. Maybe the day hadn't been a disaster after all.

FOURTEEN

The worst part of it was that the shabti itself couldn't tell her all that she wanted to know. How could it know whether or not it had made her look like a total dork? Obviously it couldn't, unless one of Tee's teachers or classmates had told it so. Tee scowled. She supposed she would have to ask it to repeat to her every word that every single person had said to it. When she heard Charles and the shabti down in the front hallway, Tee opened her door to listen.

Charles sounded impatient. "What do you mean, 'What does "stuck-up" mean?' You *know* what it means."

After a pause, the shabti said, "Why did the girl Connie call me that? I don't understand."

Charles sighed. "What d'you expect? You hardly ever smile. They think you don't like them. 'Snooty Tee Woodie.'"

Tee, leaning out to peer over the railing, saw her brother snatch at the shabti's hair. It stepped neatly aside.

As they reached the stairs, Tee backed away and pulled her door to, leaving only a narrow crack to see through. Charles came first, the shabti close behind. It stepped briskly upward, *step-step-step*, as ticktockish as a metronome, not in Tee's nervous scurry. How could anyone not notice that?

At the top of the stairs, Charles headed straight into the library. There was the sound of a *thunk!* as he shrugged his backpack onto the bench beside the door, then he stuck his head out again. "Well, come on. Do you want me to show you, or not?"

The shabti hesitated. It flicked a blank stare toward Tee's door.

"Come on, the computer won't bite you."

The shabti's blankness was wiped away by another sudden grin. This one stayed for all of a second. "Maybe." It turned toward Tee's door. "But the paper is in the—my—backpack."

Tee slipped behind her door as the shabti entered, and pushed it quickly shut. "Show you what?" Tee demanded in a whisper. "What paper?"

The shabti gave her a deep nod. "My Princess, your servant has completed all of your homework on the bus, except that for the English class. The boy Charles has offered to demonstrate how to put the story into your magical device, the new one you call a com-pooter. He tells me that it will be easier to correct it there."

"It's 'computer,'" Tee corrected automatically. "But—"

The shabti unloaded the backpack onto the table. Fishing a paper out of one book, it held it out and bowed again. "Do you wish me to learn how to operate the computer device?"

"*No!* No, I'll go." Tee snatched the paper. "You go back in your box," she whispered over her shoulder as she opened the door and slipped out.

In the room behind her, the shabti took the social studies book from the backpack, sat down at the table, removed the bookmark from the page headed *The Viking Discovery of America*, and read on rapidly, turning the pages as quickly as its fingers could move.

Tee read the English assignment on her way along the hall. At the top of the sheet of paper was printed, *"Tell your favorite story in one page, in your own words. You have the rest of the period."* At the very bottom was printed, *"Homework Assignment: Take what you have written, and make it better, but do not make it longer than one page."* The title of the shabti's story was "The Green Stone Fish." Tee read quickly.

In the doorway of Great-uncle Bass's library, she looked up and said, "I've decided. Forget it, Charles. It's easier to write by hand. Besides, I'm tired."

Charles grinned. "I heard you had a weird day. Roger said Mr. Duran couldn't get you to shut up once you got started on how they had central heating and running water in ancient Rome two thousand years ago. Some girl on the bus said you stood on your head in gym class, too. But the computer isn't work." He gave her a crafty look. "You can read stories on the Internet. You can see movie previews, maybe even see whole movies."

Tee hesitated. The computer corner in the school library had only six computers, and she had only one turn at working on one. They were old models, like the ones in their old school. To start writing, all you had to do was type in two letters as a sort of key, and *go*. The Woodies' new one was scary. Just getting to a writing page was like playing a game that was half hopscotch and half find-your-way-through-the-maze. Still—if Charles was right, and you could read stories and see movies on the computer . . .

"Okay."

Once Tee had learned all of the steps to follow to get to a blank computer page, she typed out "The Green Stone Fish" carefully with her two forefingers. The Pharaoh in the story was bored, so he had the most beautiful maidens in the kingdom row him up and down the lake, singing as they rowed. Suddenly one maiden stopped rowing, and the others stopped, too. "Row on!" the Pharaoh ordered, but the maiden only sobbed, because the beautiful green stone fish tied in her hair had fallen into the water. The Pharaoh called for his Chief Reader. The Chief Reader called for the Chief Magician, who began to recite spells. His magic piled all of the water from one side of the lake on top of the water on the other side, and there in the mud on the bottom of the empty side lay the green stone fish. The maiden was delighted; the Pharaoh was pleased; the magician put the water back; and the maidens rowed on, singing.

Tee typed the period at the end. After Charles showed her how to move the mouse from *File* to *Save* to *Print*, she printed it out and read it again. "How can I make it better?" she asked out loud. "It's too good."

Charles stared at her. "Did somebody press your Up button this morning? Or did you just stick your finger in a light socket?" He cocked his head. "Your hair sure looks like it. It was okay a couple of minutes ago. How'd it get so messed up so fast?"

Tee gave him a wary look. "What do you mean, my 'Up button'?"

Charles came to peer at the screen. "Just that you've been"—he shrugged—"different. And your story *is* good. Is it from one of Great-uncle Bass's Egyptian books?"

"Er, no," Tee said hastily. "It's made up." She quickly typed over the words "Pharaoh" and turned him into "King."

"Why'd you do that? That doesn't make it better," Charles said. "Just more ordinary."

"I don't care," Tee said flatly. "I like it better. I'm— I'm tired of Egyptian stuff. Besides, it makes it more like a fairy tale. How do I print it out?"

Charles pointed, and Tee steered the mouse arrow unsteadily up to click on the little printer icon. When "The Green Stone Fish" popped out of the printer, she snatched it up.

"Thanks," she muttered as she whisked out the door, leaving Charles wearing a half-suspicious, half-puzzled frown. In her room, her finished math and history and geography homework was set out neatly side by side, and the little wooden shabti was back in its box. The shabti was working better than she had ever dreamed. She had almost finished her last library book, but tomorrow she would stay at home. The shabti could take the books back to the public library after school and bring her six more. There must be *some* book among Great-uncle Bass's hundreds and hundreds that would be fun to read until it came back.

"I'll set the table and wash up the dishes myself tonight," she announced aloud to the shabti box. "It's only fair."

The truth was that it would be asking for trouble to use the shabti at home anymore. It had fooled Charles, but then Charles ignored her half the time. Tee suspected that one look was all their parents would need to sharpen their ears and eyes. Once they found out—

Tee felt a sudden twinge of panic.

Her mother and father had seen it at breakfast. They had seen it. They would have said something if they had noticed anything wrong. If they hadn't, then there was nothing to worry about. . . .

So why did she feel suddenly miserable?

FIFTEEN

On Tuesday morning, Mrs. Woodie called up to Tee to hurry up and come down to breakfast. Tee turned over in bed, yawned, stretched, and smiled at the thought of the long, lazy day ahead.

"Shabti, you go," she said.

The day that followed was delicious, reading, watching the video of *Willow*, and eating. She ate leftover macaroni and cheese, an almost-full bag of corn chips, a frozen candy bar, and two bananas. Just about everything else in the refrigerator or the cupboards in the pantry was clearly meant for breakfasts or dinners, so after lunch she looked up a recipe for peanut-butter cookies and made a batch. Afterward, she washed up and dried the bowl and spoons and beaters and cookie sheet carefully and put them away. The cookies, when they were cool, went into the cookie jar. Even if she didn't finish them, Charles probably would.

They didn't taste as good as her peanut-butter cookies usually did.

In mid-afternoon, Tee changed into her school uniform so that she would look as if she had just arrived home, and opened her window wide so that she could hear the bus when it stopped at the corner up on State Road. She heard it come and pull away, and soon afterward a loud shriek of laughter. The shabti came in sight first. It was holding a paper in the air and running down the lane with Charles chasing after it. They tried to turn through the gate at the Woodies' front walk, but were going so fast that they overshot and came circling back across the lane.

Tee quickly pulled the table away from the window and dropped to her knees in front of the sill to keep from being seen from below. The voices rang out clearly.

"Come on, Teesha, give it back! I'll get in trouble!"

"What will you give me if I do?"

Then they were on the porch, their voices too muffled to understand.

Tee shivered as she sat back on her heels. Better and better, she told herself uncertainly. It had Charles really fooled.

It had even giggled.

The front door slammed, and Tee slipped out into the upstairs hallway to listen, and to watch. She stood against the wall, in the shadows, where she could see down between the heavy oak balusters that supported the handrail along the hall landing.

"C'mon," Charles was saying. "It starts at four-thirty, and it's one you like: *I Was a Sixth-Grade Alien.*"

"No, I don't think so," the shabti said. Its back was turned, but Tee had a queer feeling that it knew she was watching. It couldn't, of course. It hadn't once looked up since she came out of her bedroom. "Thanks anyway, Shrimp," it said as it moved toward the stairs.

Charles vanished into the living room, and Tee shrank back toward her open door. How on earth had it known that she sometimes called Charles "Shrimp"? She couldn't remember having used that sisterly insult in weeks, and certainly not when or where the shabti could have heard it. Charles must have mentioned it, or complained about it. She watched the shabti climb stiffly up the lower stairs, then whisked behind her door and pulled it softly shut.

The shabti came in a moment later. It set her backpack down on the table and with a deep nod announced, "I have done as my Princess ordered. Shall I do the homework now?"

"I guess so," Tee answered uncertainly. "Did everything go okay at school?"

"Yes," said the shabti.

"Nothing went wrong?" Tee prompted.

"No, my Princess. Nothing."

It was frustrating. The silly stick wouldn't know whether it had said or done something totally and fatally weird unless someone told it so to its face. All sorts of things could have gone wrong. Tee wished she knew what questions to ask. *Some*one must have noticed a difference. Maybe she should pump Charles. The school was so small that if anything truly weird had happened, even in last period, everyone would hear about it between the last bell and the bus stop.

"Okay," she said discontentedly. "Go on, do the homework."

She sat on the bed and watched for a little while, but seeing her own face and shape bending over a workbook with a pencil flying through the work was too eerie for comfort.

She stood up. "Shabti, when you're in here you don't have to look like me. It makes me feel twitchy."

"Yes, my Princess," it said, and with a shimmer it was wearing its Egyptian garb again. It turned to her the blank, dark-rimmed eyes of the wooden shabti.

Still uneasy, Tee went out and downstairs to the living room. "I changed my mind," she told Charles, who was stretched out on the floor in front of the television. "What's happened so far?"

"The kid there—the wimpy-looking one—is the alien, and the tall, skinny man with the pipe and the goofy-looking lady are the ones who've adopted him." As the commercial came on, he rolled over to look at her. "He got kicked out of school for some weird stuff, so in that last bit they were taking him off to a fancy-pants school for problem rich kids."

"Unh-huh," Tee said vaguely. "You want some cookies? They're peanut butter."

"Sure." Surprised, Charles pushed his glasses up his nose to stare after her as she went out the door. "Milk, too?"

Her voice floated back from the direction of the kitchen. "Okay, moo juice for two."

Upstairs, the shabti—dressed in capris and a T-shirt—took the rest of Tee's homework, already finished, from the backpack and spread it out neatly on the table. Then it slouched down in the chair, took up one of Tee's library books, and with a swift rustle of pages, began to read.

On Wednesday morning, the shabti went off to Oasis Wells Middle School with the six books to be returned to the public library, a list of new books to check out, and money for chocolate bars, Oreos, and cheese crackers from the corner store across from school. Tee went back to sleep and didn't get up for breakfast until ten. She was still in her pajamas at noon when the sound of a car in the driveway drew her to the living-room window. Her mother had come home for lunch. The bags she unloaded from the trunk of the car showed that she had come by way of the mall supermarket. She must have noticed that the kitchen-cupboard snack shelf was almost bare. Tee told herself to try to be less hungry between meals in future. *Less greedy*, she thought sheepishly.

At least she was ready this time. *The Mask of Fu Manchu*, from Great-uncle Bass's library, a box of saltines, a jar of peanut butter, and a knife were waiting for her in the cellar in a big old tin box that had once held Christmas candy. There was a big, blue thermos of water, too. When, an hour later, the distant slam of the front door and the sound of the car leaving came, Tee put a marker in her book and left it in the tin box with the peanut butter and half-empty box of crackers. Back up in the kitchen, to keep herself from opening the new potato chips or pretzels or chocolate chip cookies, she made herself two sandwiches with the last of an old package of cheese. She could find only kiddie cartoons, and boring soap operas and talk shows on TV, so she ended up reading the morning newspaper.

The shabti and Charles were not on the 3:55 bus. Or the 4:55. They came at a quarter to six in the car with Mr. and Mrs. Woodie, the shabti with the new library books, the sack of snacks, and all of Tee's homework already finished.

"Your servant has joined the Afterschool Art Club," it explained when Tee shut the bedroom door behind it. "It was the boy Charles's idea. He came with your servant to the library afterward and then, because it was late, to the shop. Your homework is done. I shall go down to sit the table now."

"'Set'," Tee corrected snappishly. "And *I'll* go down."

It was silly to be jealous of a stick of wood, but she was. The Afterschool Art Club! She had longed to join the Art Club, but didn't go for fear she wouldn't be any good at it. Now, setting the table, she banged the silverware down, and poured the glasses of water so impatiently that she had to mop up after herself with a tea towel.

On Thursday, Tee awoke with a miserable headache. She had meant to go to school for herself, but couldn't even drag herself as far as her closet. She groaned out, "Shabti, go to school," and stumbled back to bed to pull the covers over her head.

By lunchtime she was feeling much better—enough better to make a thick ham sandwich for her lunch, but not enough to finish it, or to read. She went back to bed and slept again. When she awoke, her clock said three-thirty. She lay in bed trying to decide whether

her head really felt as good as she thought it did. When she heard the gate clang, and the sound of excited voices, she pushed herself off the bed and went to the window to peer out from behind the curtains. There was Charles, doing his backward hop up the walk, waving his arms and talking excitedly—as usual. Coming after him were the shabti-Tee, Anjali Gupta, and Poppy Cardenas from Charles's homeroom.

Tee stared. Anjali—her father was a doctor—lived in town in the large house on Cross Street where he had his office, Poppy lived almost next door to the school, but here the two of them were. Why? Their talk was so excited, all four overlapping each other, that even when they were right under the window, Tee could make out only snatches.

" . . . and Connie's dad has . . ."

" . . . can do it up like a haunted . . ."

" . . . have decorations . . ."

" . . . dead body on the front porch . . ."

" . . . and I can bring . . ."

The front door slammed, and there was nothing more to hear. The voices moved into the living room, where they were only a murmur. She didn't dare creep down the stairs to listen beside the open doorway, because if anyone came out, she would be stuck. There was no way she could duck into the kitchen or across the front hall to the dining room without being seen.

And what if they came up to her room? Muttering angrily to herself, she dragged a chair into the closet. She ought to be down in the living room her*self*. And why would Anjali and Poppy want to be with that— that *stick* in the first place? When she had changed from her pajamas into a just-home-from-school T-shirt and flowered shorts, Tee sat in the closet, with the light on and *The Secret of the Old Tower* to read, for almost an hour. It felt like three hours. What were they doing? What could they be talking about? Tee felt sorrier for herself and more trapped every minute.

When at last she heard the dim sound that was the heavy front door banging shut, she slipped out and across to the window. She was in time to see the two girls close the gate and hurry up the lane toward the bus stop. At the sound of footsteps in the hallway outside, she darted back into the closet and peered out through the crack along the hinge side of the half-open door.

She saw the shabti step in and close the door swiftly behind it. It gave a hasty nod as Tee appeared, then blinked, put its hands together, and nodded again. "Here I am, my—"

"Oh, be quiet and go back in your"—Tee snapped— "no, *don't*," she said suddenly, and took a deep breath. "Why didn't you—why were those girls here?"

This time the blank-faced shabti made a real bow, not a nod. "They and you and the boy Charles are to plan the feast for the dead—a Halloween party, they call it—for your classes."

"Oh, go back in your box," Tee said grumpily, and slammed out the door.

The rest of the story came out at dinner without Tee having to say more than a word or two. Charles, a fast swallower, was an expert at eating greedily and talking at almost the same time. Tee, who never had much to say at the dinner table, was always the one who got reminded about not speaking with her mouth full.

" . . . and Tee's in charge of decorations," Charles said with a wave of a forkful of green beans.

Both of their parents were suddenly more interested. They were surprised, too, Tee saw, though they tried not to show it. "That's great, Tee." Her father beamed. Her mother opened her mouth to say something, too, but Charles was off again.

"I said we ought to do a Haunted House, and have it here. There are just our two classes," he announced. "The house isn't as creepy as when it was full of Great-uncle Bass's junk and cobwebs, but we could do it up again—"

"With fake cobwebs." Tee made a stab at a chunk of potato with her fork. She slid a sideways look at Charles. "And a body on the front porch."

"And heavy old curtains across the dining room doorway," Charles went on, "and a coffin on the table with a dummy in it, with the food all around. Poppy says we can borrow the old dummy that used to be in the front window at the cleaner's shop. And Tee has a whole list."

Mr. and Mrs. Woodie looked at each other.

"It's a great idea," Mr. Woodie said with a grin. "I seem to remember that your mom has a tasty recipe for French-fried worms. Fake ones, of course," he added as Charles choked in mid-swallow.

Mrs. Woodie wore an absentminded look, as if she were already busy dreaming up treats like grape eyeballs in Jell-O or chocolate-covered Rice Krispies bones. "It's a good thing we have almost two weeks to get ready," she said thoughtfully.

Tee was beginning to think so, too. Tomorrow—

Tomorrow she was going to go to school for herself.

SIXTEEN

Tee awakened in the dark, and fuzzily wondered why. The alarm clock hadn't buzzed. The house was quiet. She turned over and went back to sleep.

The next time she awoke, it was still dark. She lifted her head to peer toward the clock, and was puzzled to see a thin, bright line of light shining through the curtains at the level of the windowsill. She stumbled out of bed to open the curtains and raise the blind. Funny. She didn't remember pulling down the blind. Outside, sunshine glared back at her. She looked at the clock.

8:45.

The alarm button had been pushed down. The shabti was gone.

Tee began to be angry.

By late afternoon, she was as jumpy as a cricket in a hot frying pan. She was dressed in her school clothes and waiting, but no one had come home. No one had telephoned. Last night they all had agreed on the China Moon for their Friday evening supper out. The shabti didn't know about that—unless Charles had been running off at the mouth again. It wouldn't know they met up at the shop at about 5:30 every Friday to go out to eat. It should have come home. Her parents and Charles would have decided she had forgotten. They should be phoning or coming home for her.

They didn't.

At ten to six, Tee went to the phone to call the shop. She held her nose to change her voice, and told Donny, the evening sales clerk, "I'm a friend of Tee's. Is she there?" Donny's answer was, "Nope." The Woodies had left at five o'clock. "Going shopping, I think they said."

Tee took a deep breath as she hung up, and stamped an angry foot. No stick of wood was going to cheat her out of dinner at the China Moon! She stalked to the closet under the stairs for her jacket. The desert air was cold after sundown.

Her new, red quilted jacket was gone. The shabti! It had never taken any of her *real* clothes before. Tee kicked the closet door in frustration, and pulled her old navy blue jacket off its hanger.

She had the old coat over her arm and was almost out the front door before she remembered the Egyptian box. She went back to snatch an old canvas carrier bag off a closet hook and ran upstairs to get the box.

The 6:10 bus left Tee at the mini-mall, within fifty feet of the shiny red door of the China Moon restaurant. She spied the family car at the near end of the row of parking spaces, and set down the carrier bag with the box and coat in it so that she could shade her eyes to peer in through a window. The sight of a PARKER'S CRAFTS label on one of the large paper sacks in the back and one from EDNA'S THRIFT SHOP AND COSTUME RENTAL on the other made her bite her lip so hard that it hurt. Everything was turned upside down and back to front. She had all the reading and watching videos and eating and lying around the house, but somehow the shabti was having all the fun.

But not for long.

Tee snatched up the carrier bag with the Egyptian box, and marched into the China Moon.

The China Moon's hostess, who stood just inside the door with a supply of menu folders, wore a puzzled frown under her straight, black bangs. "Aren't you with—? I didn't see you go out."

"I had to go back for my bag," Tee said calmly. "Please, where's the rest room?"

The hostess used a menu to point. "On the right, past the green and red trellis," she said. She nodded politely at Tee's "thank-you," and turned to greet the couple who had come in just behind her.

One swift look around the red-walled dining room with its shiny black chairs, white tablecloths, and lamps that glowed like golden moons was enough. Charles and her parents and the stick-Tee sat in the middle booth on the opposite side of the room, about fifteen feet away. None of them were looking in her direction. Tee made for the shelter of the green and red trellis with its twining plastic vine of jasmine flowers, and peered across at the booth through the plastic leaves. What she saw made her feel as if her stomach were tied in a fat granny knot.

They were having a great time.

From the plates on the table it looked as if they had ordered Chu Shao roast pork, chicken and walnuts, Eight-Treasure Duck, and double-fried bamboo shoots, all her favorites. The stick-Tee was waving her chopsticks around and talking and laughing all at the same time. Charles was giggling so much that he could hardly eat. Her parents wore grins so wide that they looked about to burst into gales of giggles themselves.

When everyone had recovered from the laughter, the shabti reached into an Edna's carrier bag at her feet, brought out a headdress for a Halloween costume, and placed it on her head. Tee stared with her mouth open.

It was a cheap, sequined headdress that was almost the twin of the shabti's own Egyptian winged gold headdress.

The straight-backed shabti made a gesture of command, and Tee's father nodded approvingly. The table was near enough for Tee to hear him say quite clearly, "Looks great, Princess! Are you having a costume contest at this party?"

"Don't know," Charles said. He wrote something, probably a note of the idea, on a piece of folded paper beside his plate.

"The midriff blouse and long skirt that we picked out should fit perfectly, too," Mrs. Woodie said. "Last night I was thinking you'd gained a few pounds, but it must have been your posture. You look so much nicer when you sit up straight, sweetie."

The shabti smiled and picked up a chunky piece of chicken with its chopsticks. It was much better with chopsticks than Tee herself was, too.

It popped the bit of chicken into its mouth.

It chewed. And swallowed.

Tee's eyes widened in disbelief. It really *ate*. She had been feeling angry and hurt. Now, suddenly, she was frightened enough to be furious. Straightening up, she glared over at the booth through the plastic jasmine. The shabti—almost as if Tee's angry gaze had beamed across the room and scalded it—twitched, and turned to look straight back at her.

Tee raised a hand and crooked her forefinger to sign, *Come here!* through one of the openings in the trellis. Then she stalked back along the little hallway and into the ladies' room.

A moment later the shabti pushed open the door and joined her.

Tee stamped a foot. "What are you *doing* here?" she demanded. "*I'm* supposed to be here."

The shabti's eyes went slowly blank, like a lamp turned off by a dimmer switch. "But I am here for *you*." She—it—spoke with a nod deep enough to hide its face. "At breakfast the shopkeeper and your cook said that you and the boy were to meet them at the shop. I obeyed. Have I not done well?"

Tee hesitated for a moment, then said uncertainly, "Maybe. But—" She fished in her carrier bag and brought out the painted box, removed the lid, and placed it on the shelf below the rest room mirror. "But I'm here now. You can go."

The shabti vanished just as a woman stepped out of one of the stalls. She blinked a little in surprise at seeing not two girls, but only one, putting a lid on a painted box. She washed her hands quickly and left. Tee pulled a plastic bag out of her carrier, stuffed the box in, tied a knot in the plastic, stuck the bag back in the carrier, and marched out with it to plump herself down beside Charles. Startled, he gave her an odd, sharp look.

Tee didn't notice. All she saw was that the plates, the rice bowls, and the dishes with the delicious leftover roast pork, walnut chicken, and Eight Treasure Duck had been removed.

"Still hungry, Princess?" Her father grinned at the expression on her face. "We've ordered dessert. Your sweet banana fritters'll be here any minute."

In the car on the way home, Mrs. Woodie looked back and saw Tee holding her stomach. "What's wrong, Tee. Upset tummy?"

"No, I'm hungry," Tee answered unhappily—not that that was all she was unhappy about.

"After all you ate?" Her father laughed. "Is that why you got us to ask if it was too late to get the left-overs in doggie bags?"

Charles slid another odd look at Tee, and a thoughtful one at the old canvas carrier bag that seemed to have appeared out of nowhere.

SEVENTEEN

Tee awoke early on Saturday morning. Sitting bolt upright in bed, she looked first at the window—the shade was up and the sky still dark—and then at the clock on her bedside table. The clock read 5:25. The house was so silent that she shivered. Their old house, in Maine, had been built all of wood, and at nighttime made friendly little creaks and sighs, and groaned when winds blew. Great-uncle Bass's big stone house never said a word unless someone stepped on a creaky floor-board. She wondered what had awakened her.

Tee swung her legs out of bed and tiptoed barefoot to her worktable. Her fingers fumbled for the shabti's box as her eyes grew used to the dim starlight that gleamed on the windowsill and the table's edge. She felt the plastic, the box's lid, and all around its corners. The box was still safely knotted in its plastic bag. At least, the box itself was. She shook it, and felt an object shift inside. Relieved, she set it down again. Last night—yes, well, last night she had frightened herself over next-to-nothing. After all, the shabti *was* programmed to do whatever it was told to do. Her parents had told her—it, rather—to go to the video shop after school, and they *had* taken her off shopping and to the China Moon. With a sigh of relief, Tee went back to bed, and to sleep.

At eight o'clock, Mrs. Woodie went downstairs in her slippers and bathrobe, and shuffled sleepily toward the kitchen to measure out coffee and switch on the coffeemaker. To her surprise, the aroma met her in the hallway, and she found the coffee ready, the breakfast table set, and Tee herself struggling not to make a mess of segmenting four grapefruit halves with the grapefruit knife.

"Wonder of wonders!" She clapped a hand to her head in mock amazement. "It's not Mother's Day, is it?"

Tee grinned sheepishly. "You came down too soon. Way too soon."

"I don't know about that," her mother said after her first swallow of coffee. "Way late, I'd say, if we're going to make a picnic and drive up to Lake Havasu by lunchtime."

"Lake Havasu?"

"You forgot? Charles has been pestering us for months to go, ever since he heard the old London

Bridge was set up there. We told you at dinner last night. Look, sweetie, you go stir your dad and brother out of bed. I'll finish up here."

In her relief at not being stuck indoors for another long day, Tee almost danced through the rush that followed. For the first time in almost two weeks, she completely forgot about the shabti.

That was a mistake.

Mr. Woodie looked up from packing the picnic basket. "Tee, your mom's made a big pitcher of iced tea—where's the big blue thermos? It's going to be hot up there."

"I know where it is. I'll get it," Tee said quickly. She ducked into the pantry and closed the door behind her. As quietly as she could, she opened the cellar door, found a can of baked beans for a doorstop to prop it open, and pulled the string that switched on the light below. Tiptoeing down to snatch the thermos from the floor beside the wicker sofa, she hurried back up the steps.

The door was shut.

Tee tried to turn the doorknob, but it would not move.

It hadn't seemed heavy enough to push the can of beans away, but it must have been, she told herself anxiously. The lock must have just . . . snapped shut. She was about to call out when she heard a movement on the other side of the door.

"I can't find it after all," the shabti's Tee-voice called out from only inches away. "Can't we just take some ice for the iced tea?"

Tee sat on the wicker sofa, finishing the saltines and facing facts.

It was war. The shabti *wasn't* just doing everything Tee was told to do. It had mousetrapped her on its own, and if she didn't think of something, it would keep on mousetrapping her. Something had happened to it. It had been a magical stick of wood that did what it was told to do, and now it was—she wasn't sure *what* it was. She frowned.

It knew she wasn't really its Princess Tiye.

That had to be it.

When had it stopped calling her "my Princess"? A day or two ago? A week ago? And now it wanted to *be* Tee Woodie? So what next? Did it expect her to sit down here all day reading and eating crackers and waiting? She didn't dare sit and wait. Not if she could find a way out.

In mystery stories or movies, finding a way out was simple. People picked locks or shot them off, or poked the keys out and fished them under the door. Tee could see the cellar door key in the keyhole, but couldn't jiggle it loose and had nothing in her pockets with which to poke it loose. There wasn't so much as a screwdriver or even a nail on the storage shelves, the tall wine racks, or in the empty wine cupboard. All Tee found was a rusty corkscrew that she couldn't wriggle far enough into the keyhole to touch the key. Worse, at first she couldn't wriggle it back out again, and began to be frightened. What if no one would be able to unlock it from the other side, either?

When she finally did twist the corkscrew out, she gave up and went back down to sit on the wicker sofa and think.

For five minutes she sat staring glumly at the one open door of the wall cupboards without seeing it before she absentmindedly noticed that there was something odd about it. It took another minute or two for the thought to click: The cupboard wasn't for ordinary wine storage, like the three racks against the back wall. Its shelves fitted neatly, but the empty eight-bottle rack on the lower one did not. She went to take a closer look. When she jiggled the rack, it moved easily. Then, when she pushed down on the bottom shelf, it gave a tiny bounce as if it were hanging in place, not sitting.

"You're a dumbwaiter!" she crowed.

Excited, Tee snatched open the cupboard door to the right. Looking at the machinery under its disgusting gray fuzz of dust and grease, she could make out two wheels that might be gears. Another wheel held a metal cable that ran upward through a hole in the top of the cupboard and down again through another hole ten inches further back.

Tee darted back to the sofa and pulled up the torn edge of the old bedspread to rip off a strip twelve or so inches wide. Then she tore the strip into four rags. It took three rags to rub away most of the dust and grime on the machinery. With the fourth, she cleaned off the motor, then wiped clean the On/Off electric switch and the toggle switch beside it.

She held her breath, and flipped up the electric switch.

The motor gave off a tiny burst of sparks, then whined and groaned for a moment before it gave a cough and started up. In a moment it was running smoothly. Holding her breath, she switched the toggle upward. The dumbwaiter box in the adjoining cupboard gave a shudder, and with a jerk began to move steadily upward. She switched the toggle down, and the dumbwaiter returned down to rest on the bottom of its cupboard.

It worked, but was still a puzzle. Where did it go up *to?* Not the pantry. The pantry shelves and cupboards were all in use, and perfectly ordinary. Still, the important thing was that wherever it went was *out*. She reached in to lift out the wine rack on the bottom shelf. Then she gave a tug at one upper shelf. Both came out easily, but even with them out, the empty dumbwaiter looked like it was going to be a tight fit.

That wasn't the only problem. If she were cramped up in the box, the switches would be only a foot and a half away, but that was far enough to put them out of reach.

Tee turned to the bedspread again, and ripped off a narrow strip. The ripping had frayed it along both edges, so she tied knots along it to make it stronger. Then she split one end, knotted it, and tied it onto the toggle switch. The cartons of books were too heavy to drag over to be a step stool, so she pulled the wicker sofa over instead.

Switching the dumbwaiter motor back on, she took hold of the strip of cloth, climbed up, and wriggled herself into the cramped dumbwaiter space. When she gave a careful upward tug on her makeshift cord, the cupboard gave a slight jerk. Then it rose steadily into the dark space above. Almost at once there was a bump right above her head, then a dim light and a whiff of dust. Her cupboard slowed. Down below, the motor groaned and strained until the dumbwaiter came to a stop with another bump. The bump was accompanied by what sounded like chairs falling over.

Tee put out a hand, and met what felt like the underside of a carpet. She shoved, and when it flopped away, she saw that the dumbwaiter had come up through the dining room floor. It sat, with a cutout square of the floor resting on its top, near the head of the table. The sound of chairs falling over had been two of the dining room chairs falling over as the carpet lifted under them. If Great-uncle Bass actually used the dumbwaiter, he must never have used a carpet. The Woodies had put down their old dining room carpet from Maine.

When she had dusted herself off, Tee made for the cellar stairs to unlock the door. She hurried down to lower the dumbwaiter, came upstairs, straightened the carpet, and picked up the chairs on her way to the front hall, and took the steps two at a time in her rush to reach her room.

The Egyptian box was still knotted in the plastic bag.

Tee undid the knot. She lifted the lid warily and peered in. She expected it to be empty, and it was.

The shabti had changed all the rules.

EIGHTEEN

Except for a quick break for a lunch of cold leftover macaroni and cheese and a bowl of Rockiest Road ice cream, Tee sat cross-legged on the library floor, poring through Great-uncle Bass's books about Egypt until in mid-afternoon she thought she heard the sound of the car in the driveway. Too soon. Even by doing more skimming than reading, she had polished off only seven of the fifteen books stacked beside her.

"No, no," she moaned. "Not already!" She stuck a finger in *Egyptian Magic* to mark her place, and listened. At the sound of the car door slamming, she shoved the books hurriedly back onto their shelf and ran for her room. She was on her bed, apparently asleep with an open book under her hand, when her door opened and the shabti-Tee stepped in.

Tee could feel it standing there, looking down at her. She hoped it was thinking that either there had been a spare key in the cellar, or a door to the outside. She had decided that until she came up with a real plan, the safest thing to do was pretend that nothing had changed.

She stretched and yawned. At least, looking a copy of herself in the eye and pretending—well, lying—wouldn't be as scary as doing it to a real person. As soon as that thought popped into her head, she realized with a sharp twinge that it wasn't true. She had been pretending with a capital P to everyone in sight for weeks, and not given it a second thought. Thinking of it now gave her stomach exactly the same *It-was-great-while-I-was-doing-it-but-now-I-feel-sick* feeling that she got the time she ate a whole batch of homemade fudge or—once—almost an entire half gallon of Fudge Brownie ice cream.

Worse still was the sneaky feeling that the shabti was magical enough, or may have been playing at being Tee long enough to know, to know exactly what she was thinking.

The shabti blinked, and made a deep nod when it saw Tee was awake. "Here I am for you," it announced smoothly, and then added quickly, "my Princess."

"How was the awful picnic?" Tee asked. She sat up and threw in another yawn for good measure. "Hot and grisly-grim?"

"The heat was pleasant, but boy Charles was disappointed. He expected to see a great bridge with towers, but it was low and made of stone."

Tee forgot for a moment to be frightened, and giggled. "The doofus thought it was the big Tower Bridge? *That's* not the 'London Bridge Is Falling Down' London Bridge."

"It was not the falling-down London Bridge, either. Your—his parents explained to him that London Bridge had been rebuilt more than once. The one taken down and brought to the Havasu place was only the one taken down at the last rebuilding."

Tee heard the *"your parents"* instead of "your servants" slip of its tongue, and rubbed her eyes to cover her blink of surprise. The shabti wasn't just playing the part of Princess Tee. It was beginning to *be* worrisomely human with its own blinking, and making little mistakes and slips of the tongue. . . .

"I'm glad I didn't go," Tee said. She stood up, and stretched. "I've already set the table for dinner, so I don't need you anymore until it's time to do the dishes. You can go."

The shabti hesitated for a fraction of a second, but then vanished obediently. Tee tried not to hurry as she put the lid on the Egyptian box and returned it to its old place on the closet shelf. She would have felt better having it in a cardboard box taped up with duct tape and locked in the cellar, but that would tell the shabti she was onto it. Besides, it wouldn't hold it in for a minute. Until she figured out what to do, she would just have to sit tight and keep on reading her way through Great-uncle Bass's books about ancient Egypt. She might—she made a face at the thought—*might* have to ask Charles.

During dinner, the thought grew on her. Why not ask him? Who knew what the shabti might do next? She would feel much safer with *some*one else knowing.

A little before nine o'clock, after she had checked the index listings for *Tiye*, *Mummies*, *Tombs*, *Shabti*, and *Magic*, in all of Great-uncle Bass's books on Egypt that had indexes, Tee decided to take her bath and get ready for bed early. Then she would go have a conference with Charles. She had come up with a plan of sorts, but it was still full of holes. Charles just might be able to help to plug some of them.

She was going to mail the shabti back to the real Princess Tiye.

By the time Tee was finished in the bathroom, there were still twenty minutes left before Lights Out. She hung up her face towel, took a deep breath, and padded down the hall to Charles's door. Light still showed under his door.

"Come in," Charles called at her knock.

He was in bed, propped up on one elbow and reading an *X-Men* comic book when Tee opened the door. "What d'you want?"

There wasn't time to tiptoe up to it. "Charles, when you were writing that report about hieroglyphics—did you look up what a *shabti* was? Is, I mean?"

"Sure." Something in the way she asked made Charles sit up. "What are you whispering for?"

"You'll see," Tee said warily. "Don't say anything, and don't you dare laugh. Just listen."

She told him, all in one long rush, about the shabti's appearance after he had read out the shabti spell, about the mixup in the names "Princess Tee" and "Princess Tiye," the dishwashing, the gym-class experiment, the homework, the language lessons, the not-going-to-school. Everything.

"And Friday night at the China Moon? That was her—it—until it went to the rest room and I put it back in the box. I've got to get rid of it somehow, and the only way I can think of is to find out where the real Princess Tiye's mummy is, and send her there, but I can't find out where that is. I've looked in all of Great-uncle-Bass's books on Egypt—the ones that have indexes—and I found a Queen Tiye, but she wasn't a daughter of a pharaoh. She married somebody who became Pharaoh." Tee gave her brother a quick, uncertain look. "I thought maybe you could help me look."

Charles stared at her goggle-eyed, as fascinated as he was suspicious. "Why are we whispering? You're pulling my leg, right? I mean, you've been kind of weird for weeks—*good* weird—but that story's *weird* weird."

"You think I don't know that?" Tee hissed. "But I'll show you. There's time. Come on."

Charles looked at his sister as if she had suddenly grown antlers or turned purple, but he swung his legs out of bed, scuffed his feet into his slippers, and followed her. Outside her door she signed for him to stay put. She slipped inside, leaving the door open just a crack. He heard her rummaging in the closet, then she brought out the box, set it on the table, and went to sit on the edge of her bed.

"Shabti," she said, "I need you."

"I think you're nuts," Charles said from the hall.

"Shabti," Tee said, more loudly, "I found the soup tureen we used at supper out on the kitchen counter, and had to put it away. It goes in the bottom-right pantry cupboard. Do you hear me?"

Still, nothing happened. Tee didn't try again, but went to the door. "Forget it," she said, and shut the door in Charles's face.

Charles had been trying hard to hold back a fit of the giggles, but as he stood there in his pajamas, his grin turned to a frown. Tee had turned as pale as the time in July when she had fainted from heat exhaustion. He turned to make his way slowly back along the hallway toward his bedroom.

At the door to Great-uncle Bass's library, he paused, then opened the door, reached in to switch on the light, and went in. Going directly to the middle shelf on the left-hand wall, he pulled out a thin book in a faded green binding. Then he sat down at the library table and turned on the computer.

At breakfast the next morning, Charles kept sneaking looks at Tee whenever she was looking somewhere else. Except for not having a single wrinkle in her white blouse, and finishing her cereal and her stewed prunes down to the glaze on the bowls, she looked perfectly normal. She was—perhaps—too cheerful for a school morning, but for the last two weeks she hadn't grumbled her way through a single weekday breakfast. Now she was her old, grumpy self only on weekends.

"Daddy, can I catch a ride home from the shop this afternoon?" she asked suddenly. "I want to go see what books the library has on Halloween. For more decoration ideas," she added.

"Sure thing, Princess," Mr. Woodie folded up the front section of his newspaper and stuck it in his jacket pocket. He looked at his watch. "Time you two were out the door, isn't it?"

There was the usual scramble to put dishes in the sink, shrug on backpacks, then bump back through the swinging kitchen door to collect lunch boxes. Charles and Tee were out the door and on their way along the front walk when Charles suddenly stopped.

"I forgot my English book! I must have left it up in the library." He turned back to the house, calling over his shoulder, "You go on. I'll catch up before the bus comes!"

Once inside, Charles closed the door silently. He could hear his parents talking in the kitchen, so he tip-toed across to the stairs and up, and along the hall to Tee's door. Feeling self-conscious and silly, he almost turned around and went straight back downstairs. Instead, he put his hand out to the doorknob, took a quick breath, and turned it.

The room was dark, but enough sunshine seeped in under the window blind to see by. Charles peered in, blinked, and stared.

Tee's crazy story was true. She wasn't on her way to the bus stop. She lay curled up on her side in her own bed with the blanket thrown off, and her arm hanging over the edge. Charles shivered and stepped closer to peer at the alarm clock. The hands pointed to 5:15.

He had no time to stand and gape. He reached into his pocket, brought out a safety pin and a slip of paper with a note he had felt silly writing even "just in case."

He unfolded the paper, pinned it to Tee's pillow, and hurried out and downstairs to dash for the bus.

"*I have an idea. Maybe,*" the note read. "*Will tell you this afternoon. Eat this note. (joke!)*"

Tee found the note when she awoke. She scrambled over to raise the blind, and when she had read it, did a little hopping barefoot dance of relief. Almost everything that made Charles such a pain was exactly what she needed: his nutty imagination, for one thing. And when he was tracking a fact or a new addition to one of his collections, he was a skinny little bloodhound with a sharp nose and squinty eyes that never lifted from the trail.

Half for the joke, and half afraid to leave it in her wastebasket, she took the note downstairs with her. In the kitchen, she poured out a bowlful of Honey Crunch, then tore the note into small bits, sprinkled them over it, stirred them in, poured on milk, and ate it.

NINETEEN

Tee itched to know what Charles had an idea *about*. Did he think she was just going to sit and wait?

While she tried to think of something useful to do all day, she put her cereal bowl and juice glass into the kitchen sink. Frowning, she thought about indexes. Whoever made the list of names and subjects for a book's index couldn't list everyone and everything, so reading through them to find Princess Tiye wasn't the answer. Something about her tomb could still be in one of them. She felt like kicking the cupboard door under the sink. She was going to have to begin again and skim her way through every single book about Egypt. Starting now.

"Just great!" she muttered in disgust.

The trouble with skimming, even for Tee, who was good at it, was that even in the driest and dullest book something would pop up to catch her attention and slow her down. She knew how to concentrate, run her eyes down a page without quite focusing on it, and let the word or name she was looking for just jump up at her. Still, every once in a while she found herself slowing down to read about tomb robbers, or how to make dead bodies into mummies, or how little children all ran around without any clothes on, or that there had been black pharaohs and women pharaohs.

She took fifteen minutes off from skimming at noon for a peanut-butter-and-jam sandwich and a glass of milk, and headed back upstairs.

The skimming turned up Queen Tiye several times, but nothing about her tomb or where her mummy might be.

At two o'clock, Tee returned the last book to its shelf. From where she sat cross-legged on the library floor, she scowled at the computer sitting on the long oak table across the room. She stood and stretched her half-numb legs. The book lying beside the computer keyboard was her father's *GoGlobal for Nitwits*, and Tee drifted over to frown down at the corny cartoon of a wild-haired man sitting in front of his computer and chewing his fingernails. After a moment, she sat down on the desk chair and pulled the book toward her.

Turning on the computer, she went slowly on from there, biting her lip and following the directions in the book with a careful forefinger. When she had typed and clicked her way to the GoGlobal Sign-on box, she found *Frank*, *Sally*, and *Charles* on the user list. By then it was, amazingly, past 2:30. Instead of taking the time to follow the steps that it would take to enter her own name, she clicked on Charles's.

The explosion of fireworks followed by *You're On!* startled her. A little mailbox in the middle of the screen popped open to show a letter inside, and then swooped up to the left-hand corner. The words *You've Got Mail* winked on beneath it. She was tempted, but decided not to snoop. She didn't want to get on Charles's wrong side, not now—and who knows? She wasn't sure, but the next time he checked his mail, he might be able to tell someone else had opened it first. It wouldn't be hard to guess who.

Instead, she turned to the list of search words in *Nitwits*, and tried *Egypt* first. From the choices on *Egypt*'s home page, she picked *Exploring Ancient World Cultures* and clicked on *Egypt* there, too. That home page didn't give many choices, and the only one that had anything to do with the Afterlife or mummies was *The Book of the Dead*. She had already skimmed that, so she went back to the search words list and decided to try *Museums*. That trail led from *Art Museums* to *African*, but nothing was listed for *Egypt*. She tried the search word *Art History*, clicking from *Art History Network* to

Civilizations to *Egyptian Art*, and from there to *The New Kingdom*, which turned out to be a dead end. So were *The Old Kingdom* and *The Middle Kingdom*. Each of the pages said, "Add your site to the Art History Network," but nobody had added one. In disgust, Tee clicked on the *EXIT* button and then clicked herself back out to the *You've Got Mail* screen. Her mouse arrow hovered over the *EXIT* button, then shivered and swooped up to click on the little mailbox, and then *Read*.

Charles's only e-mail message listed was from someone named Melliland. Its subject was *TIYE, TEYE, TIO, TIW*. She clicked the message open and read it swiftly.

Yes!

Tee had always made fun of Charles's fizzy excitement when he solved the riddles that were the clues in one of his computer games. Now she felt a fizzy tingle herself, a buzz that went all the way to her toes. But, pleasant fizz or no, she was frightened. She hadn't thought about it before, but the top edges of all Great-uncle Bass's books on Egypt except the dictionary and the *Grammar* should have been as dusty as all the rest of the books on his shelves. Every one that she had looked at last night and today was clean. Someone had been reading them. If it had been Charles . . .

What if it hadn't been? Tee switched on the printer and clicked on the *Print* button. As soon as the printout dropped onto the printer's Out tray, she clicked on *Delete*, and the message vanished. As quickly as she could, she clicked herself all the way out to the blank, black screen, switched off the printer, folded up the paper, and stuffed it into her pocket.

The clock on the library wall read 3:30.

No one came until almost 6:00.

Tee, listening and watching at her window, jumped at the sound of every car or truck that passed along State Road up at the end of the lane. When, just before six, the family car turned in at the driveway, she drew back behind the curtain to watch. Charles and the shabti-Tee—where had they been?—scrambled out of the back seat and vanished beneath the porch roof. A few moments later, the front door banged shut. Charles loved to bang it because it was big and heavy, and made a boom like a door in a *Dracula* movie castle.

When the shabti sailed into Tee's room, Tee was on the bed pretending to read the October *National Geographic*. The shabti emptied her backpack onto the table and began to arrange everything neatly.

"I've brought us more books from the library," it said. "I don't like the library—it's too cold—but I finished our homework there, too, while Charles and I waited until time to go to the video shop."

"Good," Tee said weakly. She was frightened by the new "us" and "our." The sooner it was in its box, the better, so she said quickly, "It's Charles's turn for kitchen duty tonight, so I won't need"—she stopped as the shabti moved toward the door—"where are you going?"

"Just down to the kitchen. I'm thirsty."

Thirsty? In her alarm, Tee forgot caution. "I was *going* to say I don't need you anymore tonight. And you don't *get* thirsty."

"Oh, but I do." The shabti spoke calmly, but its dark eyes glittered. It moved away from the door. "I'll be right back up. You wait here."

Tee's mouth opened in surprise as the shabti reached out and touched her. And then, suddenly, she was in the dark.

She was in a dark, closet-like space too narrow to sit down in, and with a ceiling close overhead. The walls were unpainted wood, and the wood had a familiar, musty smell.

It was the Egyptian box.

TWENTY

Not even the worst nightmare Tee had in her whole life had been so scary. She looked up at the sliver of light close overhead and was thankful that the lid wasn't airtight. She reached up and pushed. The lid wasn't airtight, but it fit too snugly for her to budge it. She shut her eyes and tried desperately to think.

She hadn't seen this coming. How could she? She should have stopped the game once she realized the shabti wanted to *be* her, but even by then it was probably too late. It had stopped *being* a game.

Charles. There was still Charles. Tee's frightened giggle turned into a hiccup as she tried hard to keep from crying. *Charles, HELP!*

Charles, carrying his backpack by a shoulder strap, was waiting downstairs in the front hall. He moved to the foot of the stairs when he saw Tee come out of her room. "Are you okay?" he asked. "Where is it?"

It looked down at him blankly over the heavy railing along the upstairs hallway. Then it answered, "Of course, I'm okay. Why wouldn't I be? And where is what?"

Charles blinked as it passed him. "Your shabti. You said last night . . ." He stopped. Suddenly uneasy, he crossed his fingers behind his back and finished the sentence with ". . . you promised you'd let me look at it again to try to figure out the letters I couldn't read before."

The shabti turned and gave him a long, thoughtful look. Then, "No," it said.

Charles put on his puppy-dog look. "You *promised*."

"I said 'no,' Charles."

Charles pushed his chin out, bulldog-fashion. "I'll tell Mom and Dad you promised," he threatened.

It stood looking at him for so long that Charles felt the hairs on his arms and the ones on the back of his neck shiver up. Then, unexpectedly, it looked away and gave a little shrug. "I'll go get it. You wait here."

"That's okay. I'm going up, anyway." Charles hoped he didn't sound as nervous as he felt as he followed the shabti-Tee up the stairs. His knees seemed strangely wobbly, but he kept close on its heels as it turned down the hall toward his sister's room. He jumped backward as it suddenly wheeled around to face him.

"You wait here!" it commanded sharply. Opening the door with a jerk, it went in and slammed it after itself.

Charles waited.

It was three or four minutes before the door opened again, but it felt like forever. When it did open, it was only by a crack.

"Charles?"

Tee peered out through the crack. When she saw Charles, she opened the door wide and rushed out past him, carrying the shabti box with the wooden shabti in it. The lid was off, and she held it out in front of her in both hands, as if it contained a small, mean animal with very sharp teeth.

Charles followed along the hall to his own room. "What happened? Where's the lid?"

"It put *me* in the box. I don't know how, but it did. Why did it let me out again? Did you make it? You did, didn't you? What about the lid? Oh—I left the lid off so I can be sure it's really in there." She gave a shudder and set the Egyptian box down on the corner of Charles's desk, but couldn't stop talking.

"It put me in the *box*," she repeated, still amazed. "I thought it just wanted to keep me here at home and be me away from here, but that's not it. It wants to be me, period." She sat down on the bed to catch her breath and went on with a shiver.

"I guess I knew all the time that it would catch on that I wasn't really its princess and this wasn't Egypt. Not even with palm trees and the desert and river to help fool it. It learned too fast. But I didn't think it would turn into some kind of a Frankensteiny monster. Well, not a monster, exactly. It just wants to be real."

"Look—" Charles said. He wondered whether he ought to pinch himself, as if there was a chance the whole story was a dream he might wake up from at any minute. "You wanted to mail it back to where it belonged. So let's find out and do it."

"It's not that easy. That's why I"—she fished the e-mail printout from her pocket and thrust it at him—"that's why I erased this out of the computer after I snooped and found it. The stick's probably learned how to read e-mail, too. This is from that professor you wrote to about the hieroglyphics, isn't it?"

Charles nodded as he read. "He says Tiye and Teye and a Tio and Tiw *were* all princesses, but only Tiw wasn't grown up when she died."

Tee nodded. "And nobody knows where Tiw is. I read in one of Great-uncle Bass's books that they found lots of mummies in Egypt nobody knows the names for. I guess the only place to send the shabti off to is the Egyptian Museum, but it's too late. That thing can get out of the box anytime it wants to. If you weren't here, it would. We could mail it anywhere—to the South

Pole, even. It would pop out of the box before we left the post office."

"Maybe. Maybe not." Charles reached into his backpack to pull out a thin book. He held it out to her. "I took it to school with me just to be safe."

"*Spells and Spellings: Egyptian, Assyrian and Persian Magic*? Oh! Great-uncle Bass wrote it! It says, '*By Sebastian Fall.*'"

"Look there where I put the marker. Halfway down the page."

Tee found the place and began to read aloud from where Charles pointed:

> "*'The Egyptian worker of magic knew that the creatures raised by a spell could cause unforeseen harm, even great danger to the deceased. For protection from such perils, he needed only to mutilate certain hieroglyphs. Removing one leg from each bird hieroglyph, and severing snakes' heads from their bodies would make the spell safe.'*"

Tee looked up. "That's all? It's that easy? How would we do it?"

Charles considered. "Scrape those bits of paint off? Maybe if you're careful, you can take off the black paint, and not the white underneath."

Tee jumped to her feet and pushed the box across to Charles. "You do it. I don't want to touch it. You're used to working on those itty-bitty soldiers, so you'll do it better anyhow. I'd make a mess of it."

Charles nodded and opened the desk drawer that held his shoe box full of pens and paints and brushes. He rooted around in the box and brought out an X-Acto knife. Taking the wooden figure from the box, he placed it flat on the desk, pulled his magnifying-glass lamp close, and began delicately to scrape away at first the front legs of two quail chicks, then two owls, another quail chick, and two more owls and a vulture. The cobra in the next-to-last line was last.

"Some of the white paint came off in a couple of places," he said, looking up. "I couldn't help it. I've got a white pencil, though. I could cover it up."

"Uh, better not," Tee said. She put out her hand. "Give it here."

Propping the shabti against its box, she said to it, "Shabti, I need to take Charles's turn setting the table and doing the dishes tonight. Please go set the table." As she said it, she backed away.

Nothing happened at all.

They waited.

Tee let out a long sigh of relief. It was only a piece of wood. It was a piece of wood and couldn't wake up, because it knew she wasn't Tiw.

* * *

"*Well*, now!" Mr. Woodie choked and covered his mouth with his napkin. When he recovered, his eyes were watering. "That's a pret-ty wild story, Princess. I think maybe you've been reading too many Jessica Jacksons."

"That's okay," Tee said. "Laugh. I don't care." She did, but only a little. She was too happy.

Mrs. Woodie was giggling quietly into her fruit salad, but when she saw everyone looking at her, she nodded toward the carton sealed with duct tape that sat on the table beside Tee, and swallowed. "That's the shabti? And you really do want to send it back to Egypt?"

"We did," Tee said, "but Charles phoned the post office's 888 number for rates, and they said it would be thirty-two dollars and something airmail, and eighteen-something for surface to Cairo. We only have eleven dollars and fifty-two cents."

"Ah-hah," Mr. Woodie said. "Are you fishing for a contribution? I think one could be arranged."

"In fact," Mrs. Woodie offered, "I'll take your parcel to the post office tomorrow when I go to the bank, if you like. I think it's a wonderful idea to send the shabti box to the Egyptian Museum."

"Mm-mm." Mr. Woodie waved his spoon until he had swallowed. "I'm sure Great-uncle Bass would approve, too."

185

"Okay, that's settled," Charles declared. He was relieved to get back to the practical, familiar matters. "Can we get a contribution for a black-light lamp for the Halloween party, too? We need one for haunted-house glow-in-the-dark decorations."

"Some plywood, too," Tee put in, "to cut out and paint for headstones in the front yard."

"But no mummies?" her father teased.

"No mummies!"

"No mummies," Charles echoed.

"We'll make a list." Tee drew a deep, happy breath. "I can't wait to go to school tomorrow!"

This time it was Charles who choked on a giggle.